THE AFTER SCHOOL CRIME CLUB

HAYLEY WEBSTER

nosy crow

To Debbie, a TA who makes a huge difference,
and a wonderful friend

First published in the UK in 2023 by Nosy Crow Ltd
Wheat Wharf, 27a Shad Thames,
London, SE1 2XZ, UK

Nosy Crow Eireann Ltd
44 Orchard Grove, Kenmare,
Co Kerry, V93 FY22, Ireland

Nosy Crow and associated logos are trademarks and/or registered trademarks of Nosy Crow Ltd

Text copyright © Hayley Webster, 2023
Cover and inside illustrations copyright © Kim Ekdahl, 2023

The right of Hayley Webster and Kim Ekdahl to be identified as the author and illustrator respectively of this work has been asserted by them in accordance with the Copyright, Designs and Patents Act 1988.

All rights reserved

ISBN: 978 1 78800 606 4

A CIP catalogue record for this book will be available from the British Library.

This book is sold subject to the condition that it shall not, by way of trade or otherwise, be lent, hired out or otherwise circulated in any form of binding or cover other than that in which it is published. No part of this publication may be reproduced, stored in a retrieval system, or transmitted in any form or by any means (electronic, mechanical, photocopying, recording or otherwise) without the prior written permission of Nosy Crow Ltd.

Printed and bound in Great Britain by Clays Ltd, Elcograf S.p.A.
Typeset by Tiger Media

Papers used by Nosy Crow are made from wood grown in sustainable forests.

3 5 7 9 10 8 6 4 2

www.nosycrow.com

CHAPTER
1

There's a photo of Gene Kelly, Debbie Reynolds and Jean Hagen from *Singin' in the Rain* on Nanna's mantelpiece above the gas fire, and it's been there for as long as I can remember. It's in a silver frame, placed next to the carriage clock; the clock that's always ten minutes fast so Nanna would never be late for anything.

Ten whole free minutes, Willow. Think of what you can do with ten free minutes!

It's not the famous photo from the movie poster: the one that doesn't even have Jean Hagen on it but has Donald O'Connor with Gene and Debbie, all three of them wearing rain macs and twirling big black umbrellas. In the rain.

Singin' in the Rain was in Nanna's top three musicals of all time. It was released in 1952 but the film was actually set in 1927, when movies stopped being silent and started having sound. Imagine that. Movies with no talking.

The other two in her top three were *An American in Paris*, which also starred Gene Kelly, and *High Society*, which didn't.

I have watched all three of them with her a zillion times.

"You can have this one day, Willow," she said

as we looked at the photo together, on more than one occasion.

I told her I didn't want it. Not because I didn't. But because I knew what me having it would mean, and I never, ever wanted that to happen. "You'll want it, I know," she'd say as she squeezed my hand. I always nodded. A little bit. Just so she knew I knew she was trying to say she loved me. But I always knew that. Nanna never made me doubt it. Not once.

Maybe that's why I spent more time here than at home. Even when I didn't have to.

Nanna had a thing about Gene Kelly. "Not as handsome as your grandfather," she always said. "But not far off."

I look at Gene now, as I hear Mum moving things around in the kitchen. Clatter, stack, bump. I wish she'd be a bit more gentle. It feels like we shouldn't be touching these things at all, let alone clumping them in boxes, and picking over things that are still covered in Nanna's fingerprints.

Evidence she'd existed.

In *Singin' in the Rain* there are two famous movie actor characters, Don Lockwood and Lina Lamont, who everyone thinks are a real couple because they constantly play a real couple on screen, but they're not at all, even though Lina would like them to be. Don (played by Gene Kelly) and Lina (played by Jean Hagen) have always been in silent movies, but now there is sound and their new movie is going to be a musical and it turns out only Don has a nice voice, and Lina really hasn't.

Don's best friend, Cosmo (played by Donald O'Connor), is a great musician and convinces the studio to take on unknown actress Kathy Selden (played by Debbie Reynolds) to sing Lina's part from behind a curtain. Don and Kathy end up falling in love and starring in movies together, without her hiding behind a curtain.

I've always felt a bit sorry for Lina, who's laughed at a lot in the movie, and who can't really help that her voice doesn't sound right. But the bit where Don realises he's in love with Kathy has him singing in the rain about how happy he is.

It's really wonderful.

The movie's very funny and has great songs and dancing in it. The scene where Gene Kelly sings in the rain is an absolute classic. I'd love to have that feeling. *I'm happy again.*

I haven't got it in me to touch the frame, almost like if it stays right there, then Nanna will come up behind me and say, "Staring at our Gene again, are we, Willow?" and playfully tap me on the arm. I never minded being teased by Nanna. It was the gentle kind of teasing, the type that comes with love and affection, and knowing exactly what sort of thing you can joke about and make a person feel safe with, rather than the other kind. The trickster kind. The mean kind. The get-everyone-in-class-to-laugh-at-you kind. The kind I know more about than most people and which I still struggle to spot until it's too late, no matter how many times I've experienced it.

We played "Singin' in the Rain" at her funeral, at her request.

It actually hurts to think of it. Of that song. Her song. Playing there without her to sing along, to do her silly dance exactly the way she always had done. The words floating, and us sitting quietly, and the closing of the velvet curtains, just like at the old movies, and ... no more Nanna.

How can someone just be gone? One day making you hot chocolate and pulling the old ice-cream tub full of Kit-Kats and Fruit Pastilles and Wispas out of the cupboard above the kettle, and the next, nothing?

I keep expecting to hear the sound of her slippers on the tiled hallway of her bungalow, for her to say, "Oh, it's all been a terrible mistake and I'm right here! Look, Willow! I'm here!"

But it's been two months now, and it hasn't happened yet. I haven't visited her grave yet either, even though the cemetery is just over the other side of the hedge at the end of her garden. Even though she used to say, "One day, when I'm gone, and somebody else rents this house, you'll still be able to visit my honeysuckle, just about. I'll only be over there." And she'd nod towards the cemetery. But. If I go there, that means she's really there, and not here, and I just … can't.

I know Mum hasn't gone either. Both of us are waiting for something. I don't think either of us know what. So, instead, we sort through her stuff, and really that involves me staring at things and remembering, and sometimes stroking the bit of the sofa she used to sit on, and Mum filling up a box at a time, getting rid of things, just … putting them in a box and then giving them away. I don't know how she can bring herself to do it.

As I think that, Mum wanders into the living room with a box full of kitchen things.

"I'm going to take these to the Age UK shop. Nice for Nanna's things to help someone. She won't be using them."

I'm agog. That is the only word for it. How can she talk about Nanna's things so ... dismissively?

"Can't we keep everything?" I say quietly. "Do we have to give anything away?" I spot the sieve Nanna used and reach out to take it from the box. But Mum pulls the box away, so the sieve, the box, and everything in it, is just out of reach.

"Willow," she says gently but firmly. "You know what I'm like with hoarding things as it is. I have too much of everything. You've had two months to pick the things that matter to you. You can have anything you like. But don't tell me a plastic sieve Nanna got free with a mixing bowl in 1998, long before you were born, holds a special meaning to you, because I doubt you even knew it existed before you saw it sticking out of this box."

I was going to say I did know it existed, actually, because Nanna used to let me sieve the flour when we made butterfly cakes, or fruit scones, or any of the other things we used to cook when

Dad left and she looked after me more than you ever did. But. I don't say that. I just go quiet. And I take the photo from *Singin' in the Rain* in its silver frame from the mantelpiece. I'm not going to risk her giving that away.

"There," says Mum as though something good has just happened. "I knew you could pick things if you tried."

I don't say anything to that either, so Mum says, "Right, we need to get you to school." And I follow behind her, and put the photo into my bag. "Don't be so hard on your mum," I can imagine Nanna saying. "She's been through a lot, and she's always worked, even jobs she's hated, to keep a roof over your head, and she really tries." It's not that I'm being hard on Mum. I know she really tries. But that doesn't mean she has to be hard on *me*.

When Mum closes the door behind us, I look back at Nanna's green front door. "I'm going to come here right up until someone else moves in," I say to her, as though she can hear me, and hoping Mum can't. "I'm going to water your honeysuckle, and make you cups of tea, and watch all the old movies on your VHS player."

Nanna never moved over to DVD, and certainly not streaming. I was going to show her how to stream movies one day, but time ran out.

"Off to school we go!" says Mum cheerily, again.

"Hooray," I say as flatly as I can, then quietly, "Miss you, Nanna."

There's a rustle of leaves in the pear tree in front of the house, a whisper in the morning breeze. I tell myself it's Nanna saying, "Miss you too, Willow," and I hug my arms around my middle, as though they are hers.

CHAPTER 2

It's 3.45p.m. on Friday and I'm still in my school uniform, holding my school bag with Nanna's *Singin' in the Rain* photo in the silver frame tucked carefully inside it, sitting in the back of Mum's car, right outside The Book Box on Hexham High Street.

This is not where I want to be.

"I can't wait to hear *all* about it later," says Mum enthusiastically. I am sceptical. I know that, often, her idea of hearing about things is to change my words after they've left my lips and before they reach her ears. School finished half an hour ago and my belly is rumbling. "We'll eat at home." Mum gives me a tight smile. "Remember, no snacks in the car!"

No snacks in the car this *week*, I correct her silently in my head. The car is super tidy because Mum got it valeted two weeks ago after it started to smell. The man who cleaned it hung a little scented tree from the rear-view mirror when he was done. "Sorry," Mum said when she picked it up. Her embarrassment at the state the car had been in when she'd handed it over showed on her pink cheeks. "Gave me something to do," he said, kindly, I thought. "I'm keeping it there to remind me," Mum said, very seriously. She didn't say to remind her of what. But I knew it was to remind her to not let it get so messy again. And that it wouldn't work.

I take a deep breath. There's no way out. I'm going to have to get out of the car and go inside. I turn the handle, step out on to the pavement, and then I'm there, on the street, looking back at Mum pleadingly one last time, in case she has a last-minute change of heart.

But. She doesn't.

The sky is one of those late afternoon striped ones, all peach and lemon, like someone's put it up there with a massive paint roller on a very long stick. Like the set of a Gene Kelly movie. For a moment I imagine I'm in the middle of a scene in *An American in Paris*, a big ensemble number where the whole cast become row after row of high-kicking dancers, dressed in all the colours of the rainbow, with hats and canes, and characters pop out from behind letter boxes and public bins and shop alleys, in perfect formation.

The man with the briefcase on the pavement sings, "You don't have to go in!" and the woman with the buggy and the two toddlers agrees, twirling the buggy around, her long hair fanning out in a circle like the umbrellas in *Singin' in the Rain*, as she sings, "Just run away!" then everyone else joins in with, "Just run awaaay!" and I, suddenly in a brightly coloured rain mac and shiny boots, skip off to the other end of the high street as the rain starts to pour and I get to sing, "I'm haaaappy again!"

Not that I'd ever sing in front of anybody. I can't even sing. I'm more like Jean Hagen's Lina Lamont who has to mime all her singing while Debbie Reynolds sings beautifully, hidden behind a big curtain. Although I don't look anything like Jean Hagen either. If I had a choice, I'd be directing the whole thing. I'd be telling the dancers where to go, and how to dance, and choosing the colour of the sky.

But.

I'm very much *not* in the technicolour ensemble number of an old musical. And I'm not even doing my usual Monday after-school thing of walking to see Nanna by myself, then sitting among the honeysuckle and lilacs under a blue sky in the garden, having a can of cream soda or a hot chocolate, and a bar of chocolate, telling her about my day.

Over the past two weeks I've given Mum all the reasons I don't want to come to this thing, and none of them have worked. She's 100% certain that this is exactly what I need to *take me forward into the future* and that is the final say on the matter because Mum cares a lot about the future in a way that feels like she can see the whole of it, exactly as it should be, everything in the right place: colours, light, people. The sky just right, the setting. The lot. *She* can see it, so it must be how things should be, *are* going to be. Like a photo she's already taken. Like a movie.

She is directing a totally different movie to the one I'm in. Hers doesn't have any songs in it, for starters.

And what happens if I want to be in a *different* movie?

Mum's thing is that she starts so many projects and never finishes them. "If I'd just finished that *insert some project or qualification here* everything in my life would be different."

She's never said exactly what it is about her life that isn't how she wants it to be, but sometimes I think she sees me as a project she's determined to finish.

"Don't worry, Willow," she says as I look back at her through the rolled-down window, "I have enough forward thinking for the both of us. Nobody ever gets to where they want to be in life by ambling about. Focus. That's the key. Effort. That's also the key."

"That's a lot of keys," I say. "I'm not planning on living in a jail." For some reason she doesn't find that funny, and I hear her tut.

I scrunch up all my features so she knows I'm not happy, then turn towards the shiny purple door, and look at the window display of beautifully coloured books with bunting and little displays of lighthouses and boats and entire galaxies. There are worse places to be sent to study after school and The Book Box is actually lovely. I don't tell Mum that though. I keep my face scrunched up as I turn round and give her an unenthusiastic little wave.

"Just imagine how you'll feel when your grades improve," she calls out as she waves back.

"I'm doing my best already," I say quietly, because it's true. "Also, I don't think grades are important."

She does a massive gasp at that and puts her hand to her chest. "You'll have more opportunities. More choices in the future…" She is saying other things, but I don't hear her, and she doesn't hear me. It's why I've started not bothering to say some things at all.

"You know I just want a job in a cinema. An old cinema, with a proper projector."

"Nobody thinks like that. Everybody wants to achieve more than that. What good will working in a cinema do you?"

"I'd like it," I say. I'm leaning down to the window, like an adult asking for directions.

"Well, if you do better at school, you'll be able to *manage* a cinema, *own a* cinema, *own a chain* of cinemas!" She's going off on one of her daydreams about me being rich and successful. I don't know where she gets it from. Nothing about the way I look says I'm going to be the sort of person who owns a chain of cinemas. My favourite outfit is my grey tracksuit bottoms and an oversized green jumper with the silhouette of a cheeseburger wearing a pair of sunglasses on it. I've had it for years and still haven't grown out of it. I like plain cheese sandwiches. I like my own company and I liked going round Nanna's to watch old movies. I like looking up the history of cinema. I like the lake at the park, watching the ripples when it rains, lots and lots of tiny taps and swirls. I don't really *want* anything more than what I've got right now.

Apparently that's a problem.

I have a cheque in an envelope for Jed and Roxanne in my coat pocket. It will cost Mum one hundred pounds a month for me to go through this humiliation, twice a week after school all through term time. Mum said I could use some of the money Nanna left me to buy a rover ticket to the old movie season at the Arts Centre to make up for it. You can see any film that's on, and they're showing them all spring. And then again in autumn. They also serve great hot chocolate. So, I will go to The Book Box, and I will do the work. And everyone's happy. Near enough.

"See you later, Mum," I say, and give her a bit of a smile.

She smiles too. She's always so busy, a whirlpool of colour and sound and bright lights, a bit like an ice cream van at someone's wedding.

"See you later, Willow," says Mum as she revs

away. I watch her drive off and wonder if I got lost in the post somewhere on my way to my real family.

Sometimes, I can't help wishing I could be the daughter she must have ordered in the catalogue before she'd ever met me, the one to go with the aubergine and grey throws on a leather sofa. The one without the stains on her school trousers. The one picked to go in the school prospectus, laughing with my friends with neat hair at the joy of algebra, instead of being the one asked to move out of the way when those kids are ushered to the front and told to pose for the professional photographer. If I'd been like that, everything around Mum would be like that too. I wonder what she'd have been like if Dad had stayed. But that was a long time ago.

I also think she pretends to her friends that I have friends. Because the truth of the matter is, I don't really have friends, and to her that's embarrassing.

It's not that I don't want friends. It's not that I don't talk with people, and a boy in my class once said my laugh is a superpower, but I don't hang out with people, or have people over. She forgets that sometimes she doesn't want people over, when she's overwhelmed and the house doesn't look like it's in a catalogue. She is embarrassed then, I think. And she thinks I'd be embarrassed, but I'm not. I think sometimes people's houses are tidy when they are feeling tidy. And sometimes their houses are not, when they're not. And that should be OK.

But Mum doesn't think like that. She wants to be the "best" version of herself all the time and she thinks that by going to The Book Box I'm suddenly going to be good at school, and there'll be all these emotional moments where I win the certificate at the end of the year, where I get put into a top set when I start high school, where I'm a 100% *winner*, and there's this montage of us hugging over a milkshake at the Radley and a post with 214 likes on Facebook to say how proud she is of me.

And she thinks *I* live in a fantasy land.

I pull my bag to my chest and reach out to open the door, thinking, *Come on, Gene, help me out,* and the bell jingles as I let out a deep breath and step inside. Here goes nothing.

CHAPTER 3

I've already met Roxanne, when Mum brought me here to sign me up, and I liked her then because she talked to me, not over my head to Mum. So I walk over to where she's sitting and slide the envelope with the cheque across the cash desk, then I look about to see who's here already.

Nobody I know. That's something, at least.

"Hi, Willow," says Roxanne. "You OK with Willow, or do you have a shortening you prefer?" She's got her hair piled up on top of her head, showing off the thick undercut she's got shaved around the sides. She has ears full of studs and bars. She has a stripy pair of dungarees and bright-pink lipstick. Her hair is bleached at the tips, and is growing dark brown at the roots. She's got a black and yellow pencil tucked behind her ear, and a thick notebook in front of her.

"Hi," I say. For a moment I wonder about shortening my name to something more intriguing, nearly say Will like Mum's boyfriend, Rich, calls me, but decide on the name I was given because it was the tree my dad proposed to my mum next to. "Willow is fine," I say. "That's my name."

"Absolutely," she says, passing me a big bottle of hand sanitiser that I squirt into my palms and rub until it disappears. Horrible slime. "And you can call me Rox. If you want to take a seat on the curved table and get yourself comfortable, Jed will bring round drinks and some handouts in a minute. Help yourself to a cookie."

"Thank you," I say, as I make my way to my seat.

The Book Box is one of those book shops that's full of colour and fairy lights and displays and recommendation cards stuck to the shelves. PERFECT FOR FANS OF STAR WARS. MAGIC AND MYSTERY! WHAT WOULD HAPPEN IF DOGS COULD TALK? There's a table with a big pile of books with a written poster that says, "Hate reading? Try one of these…" It's not that I hate reading. I read a lot. Fact books. History of cinema books. I love reading about world record attempts and about how costumes are made. I have a series of books I've read so many times I've lost count about all the directors, producers and every single person ever involved in a film, including extras who appear for less than a second. But stories. Nope. Not in a book. I haven't read stories in books since Dad left. He used to read me old fairy tales and I loved them. When he left I was only five, and I just didn't feel the same about story books any more. They made me feel sad. Like Dad took the magic with him when he left.

He lives in another country now. He emails me sometimes and we keep saying we'll talk on the phone. We keep saying I'll go to visit too. Maybe one day.

I'm not tempted by anything on that table either. One of my mum's big disappointments is that I'm not a bookworm like she is. I can't help that I like my stories on screen. I can't help that every time she points out one of those brightly coloured jackets and says, "Oh, I LOVED this one when I was your age…!" just the thought of trying to read it makes me shudder.

I know. I'm a terrible person. Everyone knows reading is good for you.

A girl who's wearing the uniform from the other primary school in Hexham – red, not blue like mine – is writing out rows of spellings in her cartoon handwriting. She does those big letters with the circles over the top of the i's. In front of her is a page of cursive, like we're all taught to do, like we're all told we won't pass our SATs without. She looks up at me, picks up a pink-coloured pencil and starts colouring in the dots. Rox appears next to her, and shakes her head a little, and I notice this makes the girl smile.

"Good afternoon, Helen!" says Jed to me, appearing from behind the Staff Only door with a tray of steaming mugs. "Lovely to have you!" He's got a big beard and moustache, bright-red cheeks like they've been drawn on with coloured pencil, and is wearing a stripy shirt and knee-length jean shorts.

"Willow is her name," says Rox, looking up, smiling and nodding at me.

"Of course!" he says just as enthusiastically. "Sorry. *Willow*," he says very carefully. "Like J.Lo?" I try to smile as though I have any clue what he's talking about but obviously pull a face. "You know. Jennifer Lopez…?" He tails off.

"I think Jennifer Lopez is before Willow's time," says Rox. "Can we interest you in a hot chocolate before you get to work?"

I nod, and say "Yes, please" because Nanna always says that politeness goes a long way, and I notice that Jed is surely the smiliest person in the history of all people, even if he did get my name wrong. It's almost like he's bought his face in a joke shop, like those noses and moustaches you get attached to glasses, because it can't be right to smile that much, it can't be *possible*. But, as Nanna said, *Never judge a movie by its poster.*

He smiles and passes me a hot chocolate, and slides a printout of an extract for me to annotate with any observations on language, while I plot my revenge on him, on SATs, on my mum and her boyfriend, Rich, who agreed with her that this would be a good idea, and on the government too, for good measure.

But, having no choice, I put my bag under my chair, sit down and ignore the knobbly oat-packed cookie from the plate in front of me. There'll be no sugar in them. They are brain food. Mum said everything at After School Club is designed for *optimum learning*. Goodness knows what's in the hot chocolate. This cookie has oats, obviously, and a bit of honey, I bet, and a magic ingredient, probably. We'll never be told what the magic ingredient is, but it's nothing any of us are allergic to because our mums and dads or carers have signed a thing revealing all the secret workings of our bodies before we're allowed to be here.

Personally, I'd rather they didn't know I'm allergic to ibuprofen, certain kinds of waterproof sticking plasters, and the rubber that rubber gloves are made of, but here we are.

If I'd been allowed to fill the form in I'd have written: *I am allergic to human beings: the sound of them breathing, and when they lick crisp crumbs off their fingers then touch something I have to touch after; when they dab the corner of their mouths with a paper napkin; when they pull the looking-in-the-mirror face, which is nothing like the face they ever pull at any other time so, really, they have no idea what they look like to other people.*

I am not being nice. I try to be quiet if I'm not feeling nice. That seems to bother people less than if I say those things out loud. Sometimes those things bob around at the surface of what I'm going to say, like fish scooping for breadcrumbs in the lake.

Now I've got my bearings I can look at the others who are here already, all with brightly coloured stationery. Here we all are, put in a room together twice a week to improve ourselves, to be better.

Maybe they're all here by choice. I realise I do actually recognise some of them.

"So!" says Rox, dabbing biscuit crumbs from the corner of her mouth with a paper napkin. "Let's introduce ourselves to Willow and talk about new vocabulary."

I squeeze my eyes shut in case she thinks I'm going to introduce myself first. It's my idea of hell. Having to talk in front of a group of people I don't know. It's also my idea of hell having to talk in front of a group of people I *do* know. In *Singin' in the Rain* Lina Lamont's terrible problem is that her speaking voice and singing voice are totally awful, so much so that they keep her silent. I feel kind of sorry for Lina Lamont. It's not her fault people don't like her voice. It doesn't make her a bad person. Anyway, when I speak I feel a bit like Lina Lamont and wish there was someone like Debbie Reynolds to do my voice for me.

The day they stopped asking people to put up their hands in class to answer questions and started picking us randomly using lolly sticks with our name written on them was the day I started sitting there with a full-on heartbeat surge for most of my lessons.

Do Not Choose Me Do Not Choose Me Do Not Choose Me. Over and over. A big pulsing heart and huge drops of sweat, like in a cartoon.

"So, I'm Rox, as you know," says Rox to the group. "I like books, obviously." She giggles to herself, but I notice none of the others laugh with her. This is interesting. While imagining how much I'd hate coming to this, I'd just assumed all the other kids would want to be here. One look at the faces and the body language tells me I'm not the only one who feels the way I do. "I like art. And dogs. And I started this group to help young people like you understand the work you're set at school and show you why it's important."

"Why *other* people think it's important," says the girl who was purposefully doing bubble writing instead of cursive when I sat down.

"You know why it's important," says Jed, still smiling.

"'Cos our parents don't want us to embarrass them," says someone sitting behind me. I turn to look and there is a boy from my school I hadn't seen come in. Brynn Sommers. He's in one of the other Year 6 classes. I've seen him by the park on my way home from Nanna's.

"Now, you know that's not true," says Rox, looking sad. "It's really not about your parents at all. We are trying to empower you."

Nobody says anything to that. Which is lucky, because as we sit there I realise Rox is expecting me to say something.

"Keep going!" she says. "Tell Willow your name and a fact about yourself. We'll finish with you, Willow. As you know, everyone else here has already done a half term, but we're really glad to have you here with us too."

"I'm Nish," says the girl with the bubble writing. "I like street art and graffiti." I nod at her.

"I'm Brynn. I like doughnuts." The others laugh.

"I'm Dan," says another boy from my school. He's in my class, in fact, although we've never spoken. It's pretty easy to go to school with someone and know nothing about them if you've never spoken to them. "I also like doughnuts."

Rox looks at Jed quickly, as though she is wondering, the same as I am, are they making fun of her? It's hard to tell.

"I'm Pav," says a boy from the other school. "I like Pokémon." I like him immediately. I like it when people aren't worried about what other people think and just say what they really love.

"I'm Jamie," says someone, also from the other school. "You might have seen me at the skatepark." I nod politely. I have never been to the skatepark, and with my lack of coordination, likely never will.

Finally, the last person speaks. She has her hair neatly plaited in two long plaits, not young looking, but the way the older girls have it. She is very confident and the others all look at her as she starts to talk. "I'm Marie, but you know that. You're in my class. I like the finer things in life. I like making playlists and I like making my own jewellery." She jangles a bracelet covered in little clay charms and smiles at me. "I like jewellery that's more expensive than this. But I made this, so…" She trails off, still holding her wrist up.

Marie is right, I do know her. A bit. She's in my class, but we never speak. She spends a lot of time with the girls who like dancing and making up routines to film on their phones. She always has a sort of bodyguard of one or two boys with her when I see her around school. Her in front, two boys two steps behind. Over the years the two boys have changed, but her position at the front never has. Like she's a celebrity on her way to buy a coffee, and there might be paparazzi at any point. Funny how you can be in a class with someone for years, and not know anything about them. I was actually once put with her in PE and she rolled her eyes so far back that I thought they were going to pop out and tumble across the floor like dropped marbles. She probably doesn't even remember.

Now it's my turn. I open my mouth to speak. What am I going to say? My name is Willow and I like old musicals and my old burger sweatshirt, and talking to my Nanna who died two months ago but is still the best conversation I'll ever get?

I am saved by the bell above the door jangling, and we all look round. There, in the doorway, a perfect silhouette of *I do not want to be here*, stands Tay Welding. Year 6, in the same class as Brynn. Once flushed a boy's head down the toilet, just for a laugh, is how the story goes. Most of her friends go to the high school.

People talk about Tay at school. People tell stories about her. I have often seen her sitting outside the head teacher's office. I have often seen her doing litter picking on the field, which is usually a punishment for when a pupil has been disrespectful to school property, or another person's property.

Sometimes, in the corridors, people pull their things to them when Tay walks past. And nobody wants her sitting behind them in assembly. I don't know why. But they shuffle along, or pretend to need to go to the toilet and sit somewhere else when they come back.

She's wearing her uniform, although nothing is tucked in and nothing quite fits. It's oversized, and she's rolled up her trousers so they come to the middle of her calves, which somehow makes it look more like an outfit than a uniform, and she's carrying a bag you could fit a person into. I gulp as I wonder if she ever has.

"Evening, all," she says, confident, chest puffed out, flicking back the gelled quiff that is her trademark. "I hope I've not missed anything important." She slides her bag across The Book Box floor like she's at a bowling alley and we are all skittles. "I've not brought a pen with me or anything, so I'll need to borrow one, Roxie, hey. One of those nice shiny gel pens if you've got one, please."

"Good evening, Tay," say Rox and Jed at the same time. "Lovely to have you here. You've not missed anything. You're just in time to introduce yourself to our new member, Willow, here. You go to the same school. Maybe you know each other already."

Tay looks over at me, as though seeing me for the first time. Her eyes are brown sparks. She sniffs, then squints a bit, nods her head, and I think, *How on earth does Tay Welding know who I am?* But. She ends up shrugging.

"Nah, never seen her before in all my life," she says. "No offence."

"None taken," I say, surprising myself. "I see myself every day and even I have trouble recognising me." Some of the other kids laugh, and Tay narrows her eyes, and looks at me more carefully. I'm sure I see a hint of a smile.

"I'm Tay. I like…" She pauses. "Lurking." And she shrugs. The others laugh, not at her, with her. Like she's said something only they understand and mere mortals like me, or adults, like Jed and Rox, could never get.

"Right," says Jed, taking back control of the situation and luckily totally forgetting about me and my own introduction. "I think that's enough introductions for now. Let's move on to this new vocabulary."

Tay looks at me again, nods and chooses the other seat at my table.

"What did she say your name was?"

"Willow," I say. "Like the tree. And like what cricket bats are made of." I have no idea why I say this. I don't like cricket. I've never mentioned that they were made of willow when introducing myself before. It must be one of those accidental pieces of information I picked up, one of the things Dad told me. He loved facts and quizzes. And it chose now, of all times, to come out.

"Willow. I like it," she says, taking the other half of the cookie I'd put on the napkin beside me and putting it in her mouth all at once. "I like cricket too. Pleased to meet you."

"Pleased to meet you too," I say, and I have that feeling. The one you get when you know things are going to be really different from that moment on, but you don't know if it's going to be a good or bad or a totally life-changing thing, or a combination of all three.

CHAPTER 4

I have written in my notebook but I'm not really paying much attention. Jed and Rox said we are supposed to pick out words we don't know from a piece of text we've never seen before and try and work out what they mean. I have written:

Is copper meaning the metal or a police officer here?

What is pease pudding and do I care?

Hang gliding – I thought it was hand gliding???

Assiduously... This is a word I don't know. Does it mean really certain?

Vomit – that means be sick. Urgh. I hate being sick.

I draw a little picture of someone being sick underneath it.

There are eight of us at After School Club. Me, Tay, Marie, Dan, Brynn, Jamie, Nish and Pav. Five from my school and three from Owl Primary. I try to make sure I know everybody's names as we read through the text. I'm trying to concentrate but it's hard because Tay shuffles about a lot, and it's not just that. I don't mind her moving, but it's the way she watches everything, like she can see stuff nobody else can. Just having her sit near me makes me feel like my skin is see-through, translucent like a jellyfish, like she can see my suddenly small, nervous heart beating, fast and red, like an overripe tomato.

I realise I've been staring at her because she mouths, "What?" at me. And I mouth, "Nothing, sorry." And she shrugs and eats the rest of my cookie.

We are looking for expanded noun phrases, we are looking for fronted adverbials, we are looking for powerful language that describes. I have highlighted these on the text too. I know what all those are. I nearly passed the last reading test we did. The just-pass mark is 100 and I got 99. I'm more here for the maths, and to improve my writing, and my SPaG in general. I am awful at SPaG. It's a ton of rules I just don't remember as I do not understand why I have to use them. If someone can understand what I've written, isn't that all that matters?

"So... Any thoughts?" says Jed.

"A ton," says Tay.

"About the text...?" Rox adds.

Tay smirks.

"Well, Brynn..." says Jed. "Any words you didn't know?"

"Oatmeal," he says. "Is that like porridge?"

"It might be... Are there any clues as to why it might say oatmeal instead of porridge?" says Jed. "Make sure you are specific. But well done, that's a good start."

"Excellent!" says Rox quickly.

"It's American porridge," says Tay with a yawn. "This text is set in America. It says 'color' without a 'u'."

"Brilliant," says Jed. "Exactly right. Remember to read around a word you don't know for clues as to what it means, just like Tay did."

Most people put up their hands. Nish puts hers up. Pav, who hasn't said anything yet other than his love of Pokémon, sitting with his hands firmly on his notepad, splayed out like frog hands, finally lifts his hand too.

People give answers but I don't listen. I'm trying to work everybody out.

Pav looks about him. He's taken his tie off and wrapped it around his wrist. At my school nobody wears ties. We wear T-shirts with the school logo of a kite in front of a cloud on them.

Tay is being surprisingly quiet, doodling big leaves and petals on her page. And skulls. Her knee is bobbing up and down.

"Good. Anyone else? Marie? Nish? Jamie?"

All three of them say nothing.

"I put *assiduously*," I say out of nowhere. "I don't know what it means. Has it got something to do with trees? I remember a word that sounds like that having something to do with green leaves all year round, and it could be that. Then again... I don't know if they have those sorts of trees in America. I guess they do."

I stop. Everyone is looking at me. I am Lina Lamont, but I've got no Kathy Seldon hiding behind a curtain to talk for me.

"Well..." says Rox. "That's interesting. Thank you, Willow. I think you mean *deciduous*. But it *is* similar. Anybody want to look up *assiduously* in one of the dictionaries?"

Dan, who's sitting next to Marie, stands up. He's tall with shaggy hair that falls across one eye. He grabs a dictionary from a shelf behind the cash desk, one that looks like it's been used quite a lot, not one of the new ones that they sell, and opens it, leaning on the counter as he does so.

"It says assiduously means carefully ... so I guess Willow was right ... in a way ... because trees have to take care of their leaves?" He smiles at me.

I smile back. I don't know what got into me. That's more than I've said in English all year. Maybe ever. There's no way I'm telling Mum that though. She'll take it as a good reason for me being here, and I'm NOT having that.

There is a bit in the passage about someone ringing a dinner bell.

"I wonder if there's a name for someone who rings a dinner bell," says Pav quietly.

"You could always look it up," says Jed enthusiastically. He's still smiling and I'm impressed with the effort he is putting in with us despite a sincere lack of enthusiasm on our part.

Pav laughs then, and turns to Jamie. "Like I care enough…"

"Someone who whacks a gong. People do that, don't they? Maybe they're called a gonger." Jamie laughs. "Someone who whacks one of those big metal gongs like at the beginning of movies. They used to have those in old houses."

"None of us would have a gonger," says Pav. "We'd be the ones whacking the gongs."

"True." Jamie pauses for a bit. "I'd whack it

really hard so they were too scared to eat their dinner."

They both mime hitting a gong as hard as possible, and this turns into them punching each other jokingly but quite hard, trying to give each other dead arms, and for a moment I see Jed's smile fall, ever so slightly, until he says, "OK! Let's pause there," enthusiastically. "We're going to have a break. Time for water!"

While the water is being shared I see the others looking at Tay like she's some kind of messiah, like she's in charge way more than Jed or Rox, or even Marie who has that sort of gliding power that comes with very long shiny hair, could ever be. Tay stands up, drinks her water like I've seen men drink beer from a pint glass, and she doesn't say anything to anyone. She is in her own universe, not trying to make anyone like her, not trying to be more than she is, and I think of all the things I've heard about her over the years. The things I've thought I've seen.

Tay Welding has won a prize for youth boxing. Tay Welding once got excluded for swearing at a teacher. Tay Welding eats raw eggs. Tay Welding locked a teacher in the art cupboard and wrote,

"The learning objective is to escape the cupboard without crying" on the whiteboard. Tay Welding flushes people's heads down the toilet, watches the water swirl about their hair, and she doesn't care who knows it. Tay Welding lives with her older sister, not her parents, because who could stand living with her anyway? Tay Welding is a mystery, actually. I have no idea which of those stories are true, if any of them are true, other than the boxing one. I wonder what it would be like to be the sort of person people tell stories about, and can't imagine it. I can't imagine anyone's ever told a story about me.

Willow Strong doesn't stand out in any way at all. Willow Strong is invisible.

When we all sit down to carry on with the session the mood is different, less lighthearted. It's then I notice Marie from my class properly, because she is looking at me and smiling. I am suspicious. You learn to be suspicious when you don't have friends. You learn that sometimes people say nice things to you just to catch you out when you respond sincerely, and then they laugh. But Nanna also said, "I don't see why you presume people won't like you. You have to give someone a chance sometime, Willow, love." So, while I don't smile back immediately, I look back at her, keeping my face as expressionless as possible. But she keeps smiling, and she sways her yellow highlighter back and forth, so in the end I smile back too and she nods. What harm can it do?

We all work quietly on our texts. There are no more questions and answers, no more feedback. I realise we've all been given different worksheets, with different questions and activities. Rox and Jed have really done their homework. Mine has a whole heap of stuff about spotting spelling mistakes, and adding correct punctuation. I add a bunch of commas randomly and feel pretty pleased with myself. If this was an old musical, this bit would have some silly-sounding trombones. Willow Strong Tries To Add Punctuation. A comedy moment.

"Right!" says Jed brightly. "Home time! Well done for all your hard work, guys. We'll see you on Monday!" And that's that. I got through it. Everyone starts tidying away, and I do the same. *That wasn't so bad,* I think. But I'm not telling Mum that.

Beside me Tay swings out of her chair.

"See ya, Cricket Bat," she says, only to me.

"See you," I say, amazed she's said goodbye. I go red. I'm not sure if she heard me as I said it directly to her back, and her big bag is slung over her shoulder and she's already at the door. I wonder what she thinks of me. I wonder why she's here in the first place. Tay Welding isn't a person I've ever thought would say yes to extra classes. Tay Welding isn't someone I've ever imagined can be made to do anything she doesn't want to do.

Marie appears beside me, like she's been watching the whole interaction. I hold my hand up to my face and feel it's still hot. "She's quite something, isn't she, Tay?" Marie says sweetly.

I nod, carefully.

"We all have a lot of respect for Tay. She makes things happen. She isn't afraid of being…" She stops there and I really want her to finish her sentence. "She isn't afraid of rules." She leans forward conspiratorially. "Me and her have become really close. She listens to me."

"Rules are made to be broken," I say quickly, and wonder why on earth I said that. If Tay and

Marie are friends, I suppose I need to make an effort with Marie.

"That's good to know," she says. "If you think like that, you might fit in here. Personally, I think she likes you. Hey…" She looks at me, closely. "A few of us here like to … sort of … dare each other to do stuff? Just for fun. Just to make things a bit more interesting. How do you feel about dares?"

This question throws me. I don't know how I feel about dares. They could be fun, they could make me feel anxious. They could be a terrible idea.

"What sort of dares?"

"Just silly things. Nothing terrible," she says, as though she's read my mind. "How about I give you a little one and you see how you feel? No pressure. Just for fun."

"OK…" I say slowly.

"OK! Yes! Well. Here it is. I dare you to bring me something that belongs to someone else but they'll never really miss. Something silly. Something small. Tay sets dares like this all the time. Silly things. Just to see who can…" She shrugs and smiles again. "It's not a problem if you don't. Some people don't like it. But. You strike me as someone who ... might. See you next week?"

"See you next week," I say.

And then I'm out on the street. It's dusk, and there are puddles reflecting the streetlights, and the blur of shop windows and headlights and a town centre getting ready for nighttime. Did Marie just ask me to steal something? Or just ... find something? I see gloves hanging on fences all the time, dropped toys, a pound coin in the gutter. Did she mean that? Do I *want* to do the dare?

Mum is already there, sitting in the car, and she looks at me expectantly.

When I get in, she pauses, then says, "How was it?"

And I say, "It was awful, but it's OK. I'll keep going." And she smiles at me a little.

"Is that all I'm getting?" she says, not unkindly.

"For now," I say.

And she reaches out and squeezes my knee and keeps her hand there, like she used to when I was little. I'm not much of a huggy person. I can't remember the last time me and Mum put our arms around each other, or she kissed me on the top of the head like she used to. Sometimes it feels like we are both living in our own little aquariums, visible to the outside world, but untouchable. Bobbing about among wavy plants and coloured stones and pretend shipwrecks, in our own carefully temperature-controlled water.

"Thank you for going," she says. "It makes me feel like I'm doing something to make the future different. I took the box of Nanna's things to the Age UK shop. We can go over again next week. There's still a month before the new tenants move in. You've still got time to pick things. You haven't got your own key, have you?"

I shake my head. I do still have my own key. I took a copy before I gave mine back to Mum. She doesn't need to know I go into Nanna's house without her. That I watch the VHS movies, and make myself snacks, and sometimes take a nap in Nanna's bed under her duvet, and pretend she's still here.

I don't say anything, and she takes her hand away from my knee. I don't mind different. But. There are some things I never want to change and the thought of them changing makes me feel sad. And I don't want things to improve all the time. I just want them to be even. I just want now to feel good, not some far-off point where everything is exactly right.

As Mum drives us home, I find myself thinking about Tay Welding. And what I could take to Marie that somebody wouldn't miss. Mum has a collection of thimbles in the back bedroom. I could take one of those? No. Not that. She'd notice. At some point. What then?

I think I like Tay. I like the way she doesn't seem to care what anyone thinks of her. I like the way she moves through the world like the main character, like she deserves a fanfare.

Maybe, I think, *we could become friends*. It is a ridiculous thought, I know. Tay Welding is a rule breaker, a lone ranger, an island to herself. But so am I, in a different way. And if I think of the way Tay looked at me when I talked about cricket bats, there was something there, I know it. Sometimes you just know things. When you're near a person and you can't stop smiling, or your heart is beating faster, or you think about them afterwards just like I'm doing now. And there were Marie's words. *I think she likes you.* Maybe we have more in common than I thought. Maybe Tay could like me. Maybe she's looking for a friend.

Maybe, I think, almost as though Nanna is saying it, *I am looking for a friend*.

It couldn't hurt to try.

CHAPTER 5

It's Saturday, and there's no school, and no After School Club, so I've let myself into Nanna's house and I'm sitting in the garden. I've got broken-up squares of chocolate, and I've shared out half for her, even though she's not here, and half for me and I've put some music on my phone, instead of her record player. It's the soundtrack to *High Society*. If she was here, Nanna would have a cup of tea. She would tap her foot out as she watched the kettle boil.

I don't go down to look over into the cemetery. As far as I'm concerned, Nanna is still here, in her garden. With me.

I like the sounds in the garden and the sounds from the cemetery over the hedge. It's quiet but there's always something. Not many cars drive past here, so it's all nature. Sometimes there are birds. You can't hear any traffic, or any people. It's peaceful. I can smell honeysuckle, and I like to look at the ivy that grows everywhere. I like the dark green, and the shapes, and the shade. On hot days you'll always find me in the shade. Nanna's garden is full of shady spots, and little dapples of bright sunlight. It reminds me of a patchwork quilt. I feel happy here. Like I make more sense here than I do in the rush of a school corridor, or sitting on the cold hall floor during assembly, or brushing my teeth in the bathroom at home, or sitting in the car with Mum and feeling the rumble of the wheels beneath me. When I was with Nanna, and it was quiet like this, things felt ... right.

"I'm going to see *High Society* at the Arts Centre, Nanna," I say. "With the rover ticket you bought me. *Two* tickets."

What would people think, seeing me talk to her as though she's still here? But it feels natural to. And I don't want to stop. I imagine Nanna smiling at me. She would make the tea in the way she always did, and I'd listen to the chime of the spoon against the Crunchie mug that came with an Easter egg in it when Mum was my age, apparently. She always made me my hot chocolate in that, if I wasn't having cream soda, and she had the teacup and saucer she saved from the teaset she and Grandad, who I never met because he died before I was born, were given on their wedding day. What would she say about the two tickets? "Maybe you could take somebody?" And she'd give me a wink as I pop a piece of chocolate in my mouth.

"You!" I say out loud. "You, Nanna. I'd love to take *you*."

I have a tight feeling in my chest. This is too hard. I know she was getting old. I know she'd been ill for a while. But she was so much of what my life is, so much.

"Well, that's lovely," she'd say. "But wait and see nearer the time... You might want to take a friend." I loved how Nanna always believed I'd suddenly make some friends, just like that. She was forever hopeful. She had had a life full of friends. Flowers, chocolates, cards, little ornaments in the shape of birds or hedgehogs on her birthday. More Christmas cards than in the rows at the supermarket at Christmas. She hung them up on silver wool, criss-crossed across the ceiling.

For the last few years she hadn't been able to get up there to stick the string up. Mum's boyfriend, Rich, had done it for her. I like Rich. Rich brings out the best in Mum. Not the shiny, "perfect" version, but the it's-OK-to-be-her version. The first time I met him he said, "I have no expectation that you're going to like me, but I hope, in time, you'll see how much I like your mum, and I can fit into your life in whichever way feels best for you." That felt nice. Not like the wicked step-parent stuff you always see in movies. And not forcing anything. He's never once said anything about what I wear, or what I do with my free time, and he got me to make him a playlist of songs from old musicals to play when he's working away so he could "see what all the fuss was about".

Rich works away quite often. He works for a high-end jewellery company, showcasing new products and designs around Europe, travelling around with a big briefcase full of beautiful things that would never look right on my wrist, round my neck or on my finger.

Nanna always said, "He is nice to your mum, and he's nice to me and, most importantly, he's nice to you." She was right. He is. I am actually looking forward to him moving in with us. He's all right.

"I haven't got any friends…" I say out loud. But for some reason Nish pops in my head. And Marie. And Dan. And Brynn. And … with the thought I had last night on the drive home, Tay Welding. *They're not your friends, Willow*, I tell myself. *They're acquaintances.*

But they *could* become friends. Why shouldn't they? That's what Nanna would say.

"OK," I say. "Nanna, in my best world you'd come to see *High Society* with me. And maybe I'd go by myself. But. I'll think about it."

I hear the leaves in the breeze again. I tell myself it's Nanna saying, "I'll always come with you, if you want me to." This makes me happy, so I leave it there and eat my chocolate.

I do so much by myself, and I'm always OK with that. I've never really thought about whether I'd like to do things with other people my age. When I'm around them, I feel like they're talking a different language, and like I'm acting in a TV show with kid characters, and my character is slightly out of sync. Although … I made Tay Welding smile. I think she thought I was funny…

I'm not sure why I've always loved *High Society*, but I do. It's the music and the colours, mostly. No Gene Kelly but still in Nanna's top three. It is a musical made in the 1950s about a woman called Tracy Lord, played by Grace Kelly, who is divorced and is getting married to a new man who seems quite uninteresting. Her ex-husband, played by

Bing Crosby, is a composer and a bit of show-off and has a ton of money, and he tries really hard to convince her to get back with him, by giving her a little version of a boat they had together called *True Love*, and by making sarcastic comments about the new husband, and by reminding her of all the lovely times they had before their marriage went all wrong.

And there is Frank Sinatra as a photographer called Mike Connor who also falls in love with her because she is the sort of woman men in films fall in love with and because it adds a sort of side plot where you get to see him staring at her all wide eyed. It's a bit creepy that bit, especially as he has a girlfriend who is my favourite character. She's this journalist woman, Liz Imbrie, who is funny and sharp, and she doesn't like all the rich characters in it and is always trying to get a scoop on them.

It also has Louis Armstrong singing and playing the trumpet, and the main guy character, C.K. Dexter-Haven, is a singer and composer in the film. So even though it's a musical, and in musicals people are always singing, there is a reason for him to be singing in this one, because his job is to actually write songs.

My favourite song in it is sung by Frank Sinatra and Bing Cosby. It's called "Well Did You Evah!" They are at the pre-wedding party for Tracy (the ex-wife getting remarried) and they have too much to drink and start singing about how great the party is, but really they are saying that the party is awful because once it's over it will be morning and Dexter-Haven will have no other chances to marry Tracy, and Mike Connor never had a chance in the first place and should really just concentrate on Liz the journalist, who never falls for any smooth lines, and that is partly why I like her so much.

Nanna's first job was in a cinema. She can tell all sorts of stories about what it was like. The sound of the projector, how she ironed her uniform with starch and made the collar so neat that it looked like it was made of something solid, not material at all. I think that sitting in the dark with her the first time I ever went to see a movie was one of the best moments of my life. She took a bag of toffees in her handbag, and we slipped them out quietly as we watched. It bothers me that I can't remember what we saw. It was a Disney movie,

I think. I would ask her. But. I can't.

It's at this moment I see something at the end of the garden, a person walking in the shadow of the hedge, along the path, not in Nanna's garden, but along the back of her garden, which leads on to the cemetery. Nanna loved living by the cemetery. She loved the peace and quiet. She loved that there were no houses looking on to hers. And she loved the wildlife.

She also said she loved that when she died she wouldn't be far from home.

My heart beats faster. There's no reason for a person *not* to be there. It's a public path after all, and it's nowhere near where me and Nanna would sit, not really, but there's something about the way the person is moving that grabs my attention. Something about the sway of the walk, and the shape of the hair, that long pushed-back quiff, that big bag, that swagger and confidence. It's Tay Welding! What's she doing at this end of town? I've never seen her when I've been at Nanna's before.

For a ridiculous moment I wonder if she followed me after school. But why would she? She barely knows I'm alive. I suddenly feel really exposed, sitting here talking to my dead Nanna, and for some inexplicable reason I duck, tuck my head down between my knees and pretend I'm not there. I don't want Tay to see me sitting here. I don't know why. I know it's ridiculous. But all I know is I don't want her to see me, so I try to make myself invisible.

I can imagine the exact face Nanna would be pulling even though I've got my eyes closed. *What are you hiding for?* And I don't open my eyes, or answer her imaginary question, I just keep them closed and wait long enough for Tay to have gone away. I don't know what I'm feeling exactly. My skin is hot. My heart is still fast. All I know is I don't want Tay to see me sitting here. I don't want to talk to her and I don't want her to say something over the hedge that's sarcastic, when Nanna isn't here to tell me it's OK.

And you don't want her to see you listening to old musicals on your phone because you don't want her to think you're weird and like an old lady. No! I'd never be embarrassed of that. But the thought is there and I know that's part of what I'm feeling, and then I feel ashamed.

I sit there for what feels a long time, but it's

barely minutes. I watch the coloured patches that drift across my eyelids as the clouds move. The flicker of red and yellow. I am in a cocoon. I think, *I'm going to do the dare Marie set.* I want them to like me, I see now that I do. And she did say "something they won't miss" so, really, it's just moving something that's unnoticed to somewhere it is noticed. It can't be something of Nanna's though. Never that.

Doesn't that mean you think what she's asked you is wrong? Nanna's voice in my head. No, Nanna, it doesn't mean that. It means that I can't move your stuff just yet. Not yet. That's all.

When I open my eyes, I stand up and walk over to the hedge and look into the cemetery, just to be sure. As I pop my head up to peer over, I see Tay Welding standing on the path, and she's looking right at me. I duck down, which I regret immediately. She's seen me. I've seen her. And now I'm hiding. I pull my head up and peer back over. She is looking at me and shaking her head, laughing a bit.

"Cricket Bat," she calls out, and shrugs.

"Um, hello, Tay," I call back, as though we both haven't seen me hide from her just moments ago.

She has her big bag with her, and headphones on, one pulled over one ear and the other one on the side of her head.

"You're quite interesting, aren't you?" says Tay.

I don't know what to say to that, so I nod and say, "So are you!" and she laughs again, shaking her head. She turns back. "I can't work out if you're the most interesting person I've met in a long time, or the weirdest. I'm on the fence on it. Guess we'll have to see." And then she walks away.

Interesting or weird? Which one is it?

I want her to think I'm interesting. I don't want her to think I'm weird. *You're not weird, Willow.* I imagine Nanna's voice. *You're unique.*

It's all very well being unique but people can't like the unique bits about you if they are on the fence about whether you're someone they want to know or not.

Then, maybe Tay will embrace my weirdness. I suppose it is a bit weird to bend down and curl into a small shape for no reason. It's not something I'd usually do. But there's something about Tay… I don't want her to notice anything bad about me. I want her to think I'm funny and clever and the sort of person she'd like to be friends with. *You want to impress her, Willow,* a little voice at the back of my head says, and even though the thought of that makes me cringe, go the colour of raspberry jam right up my neck, I know that's true.

That's decided it. I *will* do the dare for Marie. What's the worst that can happen?

CHAPTER
6

The house is spotless. Over the past week Mum has been sorting and clearing, cleaning and sorting, to the point that it now looks like something out of a magazine or an advert for a TV package that costs you over £100 a month. If someone was to turn up here for the first time, having never seen our house before, having never met my mum, or me, they would think this is how we live all the time.

I think, when it looks like this, Mum thinks this is how we live all the time.

The reason for the tidying and cleaning is Rich is back from one of his work trips away. Mum's jewellery collection has grown quite a lot since she met Rich. He loves to give her pieces that I think he gets at a cheaper price. But they're worth a lot. I've seen the brochure.

Mum always makes the house look perfect for when Rich comes to stay. I wonder what she'll do when he starts at the new place in Hexham, when he's not travelling with work, and we all move in together. Will it be like this all the time? Will Rich ever see what it gets like when he's *not* here, when he's *always* here?

I've never talked to Mum about it. It's a sort of

rhythm we've got into. House like a skip. House like a show home. I've stopped noticing the in-betweens as it builds up. It usually starts with cups and plates left out in the living room. Sweet wrappers. Washing up on the side until the baked beans are like hard little stones, and the gravy is a geography project showing the Earth's crust, showing mountain ranges from a bird's eye view.

Mum has set out the dinner things and is stirring some kind of sauce on the hob. She's bought a new set of cooking equipment, all turquoise and matching, and new pans. She's bought new coasters and new table mats, decorated with small silver stars on a background of teal. She thinks I don't know, but she threw the others out, with the old food still on them. I saw her pushing them down into a thick black sack. She orders extra thick sacks so she can throw things away other people would never throw away. I don't mention recycling and the environmental crisis. I don't think she could take it.

"I walked past Nanna's," I say, altering the truth a little, stroking the petals of the purple stocks Mum has arranged in a new frosted-glass vase in the centre of the table. "Told her I was going to see *High Society* at the Arts Centre. Played some music. Ate some chocolate." This is more information than I'd usually share but, really, it's just a diversion tactic because I don't want to talk to her about After School Club before Rich is here, and, confusingly yet fine with me, she hasn't asked anything about it since she picked me up yesterday. I'd like to think it's because she's respecting my privacy, but it's more likely it's because she's been in The Tidy Zone.

She nods and stirs the sauce. "That's nice, Willow." She pauses and stops stirring. "You don't think you—"

"Have you gone to her grave yet, Mum?" I say this so she doesn't finish her sentence. Last time we talked about Nanna properly, before Nanna died, Mum asked me if I thought I visited too much, if it was healthy to spend so much time with an old woman in her garden when I'm a young person starting out in life and should be looking to the future.

"That *old woman* is your MUM!" I'd shouted furiously. Nanna was quite old for a mum when she had Mum. She was in her early forties. Mum was in her early thirties when she had me. "Do you want me to stop visiting you when YOU'RE old?"

"That's not what I meant, darling," she'd said slowly. "I just mean, shouldn't you be spending time with children your own age, being into things children your own age are into?"

"No," I said. "I shouldn't. I like old things and I like Nanna. It's not my fault you and her have absolutely nothing in common and you've never tried to!" And we hadn't talked for the rest of the evening. Or about Nanna since. And then she'd died. I don't want an evening like that tonight. I want to enjoy my dinner, talk to Rich about where he's travelled this time, and feel some kind of normal.

"I haven't," says Mum quietly. "I'm just very busy at the moment. I've got this new course that's going to get me a promotion at work. If I get a good mark, I'll be earning more money, and we'll be able to go somewhere nice on holiday like…" She stops. I know Mum pores over other people's photos online. I know she compares the way she lives to the way other people live. When she sees foreign holiday photos, she lets out a long sigh. We've never left the country. We couldn't because Nanna needed looking after. It doesn't matter to me. But it matters to Mum. She has a tick list of what a successful life means, and a successful life means having a selection of beautiful horizons that are not in the UK to display in a neat formation for people to put hearts and wow faces on.

"We could go together…" I say, regretting it as soon as the words have left my mouth. I haven't had the courage to go see Nanna's grave either, even though it's only on the other side of her garden fence. I like to go to her garden. I don't want to see the headstone. For a moment I thought I'd like to go with Mum. But. No.

"We could…" she says. "We will." She turns and smiles at me, and flicks the hob off. The pan is still bubbling, little splutters and pops. The room smells like the Italian restaurant Rich took us to last time he was back. She lights some candles and the room transforms into something wonderful. She's made it look lovely, like she always does when she has one of her big rearranges. I don't mention that it looks nothing like it did last week.

"When Rich is here, we can talk about After

School Club at The Book Box," she says. "Sorry I haven't asked about it. I wanted to, but I know you didn't want to go. I know I've pushed you into it. It's only because I want the best for you and for you not to live like…" She stops again. Mum is forever starting sentences she doesn't finish, like all the other things she starts and doesn't finish. Nanna has always said, "One day your mum will find her thing. And if she doesn't, hopefully she'll choose fewer things, and have enough of herself to spread to the edges."

"Like margarine," I'd say.

"You need enough margarine," said Nanna, "to reach the crust. Nobody wants the dry bits."

Sometimes if feels like Mum has one tub of margarine and seventy-two slices of toast to spread it on. I don't tell her that. And I've never told her what Nanna says about her either. She wouldn't understand.

The doorbell rings, and I'm relieved. Mum is too. And I can tell she's excited. She's got that nervous energy she gets every time Rich is back. She talks faster, and breathes faster, and she tries so hard to get everything just right. I'm not sure if anything will ever be just right. She's not a director and we're not actors. Our house isn't a film set. At least, not in the between times. At least, not an old musical. A TV drama maybe. With a crime scene.

Rich is on the doorstep holding pink flowers, a bottle of red wine and a small stuffed toy otter. I hope the otter isn't for me. I don't like soft toys. I never have. I don't like all the eyes looking at me in the dark when I'm trying to go to sleep. But luckily it's not for me. He thrusts all three gifts at Mum, and then gives her a huge hug and kiss, with the presents between them, so the otter looks like it can't breathe.

I stand awkwardly, moving from foot to foot. I wonder if they'd like to have a romantic dinner without an eleven-year-old in a big green burger-wearing-sunglasses jumper sitting there like a spare part, with pasta sauce around her mouth. But Rich lets go of Mum and turns to me and smiles. "Hey, Will," he says.

"Hi, Rich," I say, and I smile too. I like Rich. He never pushes me to like him, has never bribed me with gifts, or promises, or tried too hard. He gets me without me ever having to explain myself. I think it's because he was an only child too. He once said, "Sometimes people don't want to talk about how they're feeling until they are ready, and that's fine with me."

"That's fine with me too," I said, knowing he could have no idea that the only person I've ever talked to about my feelings is Nanna, and even then, I never told her *everything*.

"Where did you go this time?"

All three of us walk into the kitchen in a line, then Rich says, "This looks lovely," while Mum opens the bottle of wine and beams like summer. "The Isle of Skye," he says. "Right at the top of Scotland. An island. It's beautiful. I'd love to take you two there. They have otters." He nods at the stuffed toy Mum has put on top of the fridge along with other gifts he's brought her from his travels.

"Lovely," says Mum. "Shall we eat?"

Rich and I nod and sit down.

As we politely fork our pasta into our mouths – we always eat politely together, always at the table, never by ourselves with the food on our laps, at different times, which we often do when Rich isn't around – I wait for the inevitable questions about After School Club. I wonder what I'll say. What I'll pick out as what Mum wants to hear. She'll notice I'm not saying I don't want to go any more because the truth is I do. I have a pang of not wanting her to feel smug. Why are my feelings about Mum so complicated?

"So…" says Mum and I feel myself tense up. "Willow started at that After School Club at The Book Box on Hexham High Street I was telling you about. She hasn't told me anything about it, of course, but maybe she will with you here, right, Willow?"

I look at my food and say nothing.

"The thing to help you with your maths and English?" asks Rich cheerfully. He is wearing a suit, like he always does on the days he gets here. Tomorrow he'll wear jeans and a T-shirt and trainers. Nice trainers, clean ones, not grotty ones like mine. But when he arrives, he's always in his navy suit and his smart white shirt, his polished shoes, and a tie with a shimmer, like mermaid skin.

"Yup," I say, and put more pasta in my mouth. Mum doesn't like it if I talk with my mouth full. Easy win.

"What's it like?"

"Good luck getting anything out of her," says Mum. "She tells me nothing."

"Maybe you're not asking the right questions," says Rich kindly, hitting the nail on the head as usual. "What's it like, Willow? Was it all bad?"

I finish chewing my food and answer. I want to say lots of things. I want to talk about Jed getting my name wrong, and his comedy features face. And about Rox's hair, and how much she loves books and thinks she can get us to love books too, really believes she can even though she can't. And about the other kids, how they don't want to be there either, how some of them go to my school but have never talked to me before. About Nish's bubble writing. About Dan and Marie smiling at me.

And I really want to talk about Tay. About the way she walked in, like no adult could ever tell her what to do, like our school uniform was an outfit she'd chosen on purpose. About her huge bag that looked like it could carry a person. About how I felt when she said *"Willow. I like it. I like cricket too. Pleased to meet you,"* like it was the start of something life changing in a way I couldn't quite describe. About how it felt to feel her fidgeting beside me, stretching her legs out, not really listening to Rox, or Jed, or anyone else for that matter.

I want to say Tay is a girl at my school everyone is afraid of. She said she liked my name. And I want more than anything, more than *anything*, I've just realised, for her to be my friend.

I make a mental note to find out more about cricket.

"It was all right," I say. "We're doing language work first. No maths yet. I learned a new word. Oatmeal. It's American porridge. The other kids are all right. Jed and Rox, who work there, gave us healthy snacks, you'll be glad to know. It's all right," I repeat. "I'll keep going."

"There…" says Mum. "I told you…"

"That all sounds positive," says Rich. "Not too bad, not too good. Just right. Like the porridge in *Goldilocks*."

"I like my porridge hot," I say.

"Don't we all," says Rich.

And luckily, that's the end of that. So we all sit quietly as we finish our dinner. I'm thinking one thing clearly above all else. How am I going to complete Marie's dare?

When Rich goes to make a work call, Mum looks at the otter and then at me. "I love the flowers and the wine," she says, smiling. "But I'm not sure about the otter." We both laugh, a little.

"I kind of like him," I say. And that's when I know I can easily do the dare. Something someone doesn't need or want and won't notice or care if it's gone. Rich has delivered me my first success at After School Club. The cuddly otter might not be the exact thing Marie meant, but it fits the dare, and I won't feel bad about it. *I'm going to make Tay Welding be my friend.* I will. I just know it.

CHAPTER 7

On Monday at school, the cuddly otter is stuffed in the bottom of my bag next to Nanna's Gene Kelly photo, and Mum and Rich are none the wiser. I find myself looking out for Tay in the corridor as we line up for lunch. I realise I'm looking forward to After School Club, and it's such a strange feeling that I don't really know what to do with it. I'm fidgety, and fiddle with things, and I haven't concentrated on any lessons all morning.

In the canteen, I get my tray with the cottage pie and yoghurt from the front, help myself to cutlery, and take a seat in my usual place right at the back in the corner. From here I can see the whole dinner hall and anyone entering or leaving. It's a thing I like. Being able to see the entrance and exit of any room I'm in. Leaves less room for surprises.

I'm singin' in the rain
Just singin' in the rain
What a glorious feeling
I'm ... happy again.

This is the first time I've felt any excitement since Nanna died. Around me, the other kids in the canteen are characters dancing in the rain too, splashing in puddles and smiling at the sky.

I can see it all. The whoosh of the water. The smiling faces. The hope. I'm not *happy*. But. I feel something *good*.

Usually, the table I sit on fills up with children from Year 3 and 4. They sit and chatter and struggle to open their smoothie tubes, and their packets of crisps, and lots of them pull out the ham or the cheese from their sandwiches and flap it about like a tongue before licking it, or popping it whole into their mouths. There is always a lot of mess on the table at the end of lunch, and it reminds me of our kitchen before Mum's has one of her big clean ups.

But today is different. Today I see three shapes walking towards me that are not kids in Year 3 or Year 4. At first I think it must be a trick of the light. Nobody from my own year, or even Year 5, has ever sat with me at lunch, and I've never tried to encourage it either. But before I know it, all three shapes have taken the seats around me and one of them says, "Hi, Willow. Didn't realise you sit all the way back here." And I realise it's Marie and Brynn and Dan from After School Club.

"Um… Hi," I say, pulling my tray towards me protectively, as though they might do something to my food, or like my tray is my own private fortress.

The three of them set out their food on the table and tuck their trays under their chairs. I've never thought of doing this and suddenly feel conscious of my sticky tray and the way I've been sitting here in the corner with the younger kids all this time.

"You going to Club after school?" says Marie. I've never seen her hanging around with Brynn and Dan at school before. Or I'd not noticed. I'd noticed she always has two boys with her. How long had it been them? She pulls out a packet of ketchup from her pocket and opens it neatly, puts a blob on the corner of her plate of chips. Ketchup is banned from the school canteen because of the high sugar content. For a rebellious act it may seem small, but it feels big to me.

"Yeah," I say. Brynn and Dan take out their own packets of ketchup and add them to the mashed potato of their cottage pie. None of the lunch staff seem to notice or care. I can't help but admire them. I might bring in my own big jar of Branston Pickle, plonk it down in the middle of the table and put it on all my food, no matter what it is. "You?"

"Oh yes," says Marie, smiling brightly. How strange that I've been in her class all this time and she's never once spoken to me. At least, not on purpose. I've never once spoken to her either, to be fair. "We always go, unless there's some other thing our parents want us to do. It's actually not as bad as it seems. None of us wanted to go at first, did we?"

"Nope," says Brynn.

"Nah," says Dan.

"But it turned out to be quite a good thing in the end really. Now… About what we talked about the other night…"

I am well ahead of her. I have the otter in my bag, and I reach down and get it out. I put it on the table between us. It still has the label attached to it with a plastic stalk, which proves it's *new*. A ridiculous thing, I see now, and probably not the right thing at all, not what she meant. But she looks at it, looks at the others, and then at me, and gives me a dazzling smile.

"Is this…?"

"My mum's boyfriend, Rich," I say, "bought it for her on a work trip. He takes posh jewellery all over Europe finding places to stock it. The otter's brand new. Mum isn't going to notice it's gone. She's not going to miss it. So. Dare done." I'm feeling pretty brave. What Tay said over the fence helped. Marie's smile helped.

"Ah ha!" she says. "A love gift! Stolen!" She laughs. "Something brand new too, and not tiny. I'm impressed."

I flinch at "stolen". Not stolen. Not that. Just … moved. From one place to another. And not missed.

"I knew you'd be into some dares. I said so, didn't I?"

She turns to Dan, and then to Brynn. They nod with their mouths full.

"I love it!" I must have had a look of confusion on my face because she says, "*Tay* will love it! She might not strike you as the cuddly toy kind, but she loves a done dare. And this was pretty brave, considering it was new. And you took it from family. She'll love that you did that."

I can't help but beam proudly. It wasn't so hard. And it hasn't hurt anybody. I've already changed my mind about After School Club. I hadn't thought about the other kids there before I went, or what they'd be like. I suppose I imagined them all being there because they love learning, or because they love books, or… I don't know what I imagined. But sitting with three other Year 6s at lunch was definitely not it.

I eat my mash with my fork, jealous of the ketchup, watching Marie closely. She has only eaten a few chips, and her ketchup is all gone. I see the Year 3s and 4s who usually sit at this table wander past with confused expressions on their faces. I realise I've never asked any of them their names.

"Well…" says Marie. She looks at the other two conspiratorially. "I think you're definitely ready for another dare."

"Yeah," laughs Dan.

"Hmmm," says Brynn with his mouth full of chips.

"Ah, Brynny," says Marie. "You'll be on board in the end."

Brynn shrugs and gives me a look I can't understand.

"Brynn isn't sure about all of it," says Dan, suddenly finding a voice now he's swallowed his food. "He thinks we might be taking it all too far."

"What too far?" I ask. I hate intrigue. I'd rather they just said what they were on about and stopped talking in code.

"Ah, it's too early to let you in on all that," says Marie brightly. "But ... you have potential."

I don't like the way she says it, but I can't help but want to know potential for what. I'm annoyed at myself a bit, for falling for the hook. For bringing the otter, even. I've watched enough movies to know when someone is trying to hook you in to something.

"Of course, Tay is the one who started it. She's the one who got us to talk to you. There's a few ... tests you have to pass to be part of it. Some of the others at Club, they could never pass. But... Tay thinks you could be different."

I puff up. I am different. I've always been different. And... Tay has talked about me? I feel my heart beat fast again.

"The first thing you should know is we don't call ourselves the After School Club," says Dan. "We sort of made a joke name. A better club name. Not everyone who goes to Rox and Jed's is part of it. There's me, Brynn, Marie and Tay, and we're ... auditioning a few of the others at the moment, including you."

I'm not sure I like the sound of that. "What do you call yourselves?"

"It's a joke, obviously," says Marie quickly. "It just shows we are not so concerned with rules that make no sense. We call ourselves ... The After School *Crime* Club."

I try not to gasp. Crime is a word I do not like and it's a word I don't want to get involved with. Some dares could be OK... Leave a lesson early pretending to be ill, lie about homework being late, see if you can have a day off sick but really just watch old movies at Nanna's on her VHS. That could be OK. It's still more than I've ever done against the rules so far, but I might be OK with them. But. Crime? What sort of crime? I don't want to become a *criminal*!

In old musicals, none of the characters I ever loved were criminals. Well, maybe in *Bugsy Malone* but that wasn't that old. And they only ever shot each other with whipped cream, which doesn't really count as anything dangerous...

"Are you interested?" says Dan. Brynn shakes his head and looks over his shoulder. He suddenly seems very separate from the other two.

He gets up. "See you later, Willow. Take care of yourself." This seems like a very grown-up thing to say.

"Don't mind him," says Dan. "He's in a huff. He'll come round. So... Are you interested?"

I don't have to think about my answer for very long. Only this weekend I was wondering if I might make a friend, thinking how much I'd like Tay to be my friend. And these people who've felt so far away from me all the way through primary school are now sitting here, at my table, asking me if I want to be part of something, a secret something. Something that could get me closer to Tay.

Am I weird, or interesting?

"I'm interested," I say, and nod. I don't add it's because I really want to impress Tay. I'm going to keep that to myself. Even though it's pretty clear Marie has noticed already.

"Great!" says Marie with a grin, standing up suddenly and leaving her tray on the floor under the table, and not clearing away her plate. It's never crossed my mind not to clear up after myself. As they walk away, I think, they do everything differently, as though there are no adults anywhere at all. I don't really know what I think about that.

After lunch I sit at my table and watch Mrs Emery write down the learning objective on the board. It's "To investigate life in Victorian London".

I think about Tay. She has eyes like little fires. I feel a creep of shame about how I hid when I saw her at Nanna's, and why I hid, but I push it away. It was just the shock of seeing her, I tell myself. Unexpected and in the wrong place. It doesn't mean anything. I didn't do anything wrong. I push the thought of Nanna's face out of my head too. I never want to disappoint her.

What would Nanna think about you joining an After School Crime Club, hey, Willow? I push that voice away too. I can't think of everything at once.

I look across the room and see Marie writing with her sparkly pen, sitting up straight, and somehow looking as tidy as she did at the beginning of the day. How does she do that? Maybe if I'm feeling brave I'll ask Mum how people do that. Mum does it too, at least when she's out of the house.

"Right!" says Mrs Emery. "Looking back at last week's drama work about the work of author

Charles Dickens, what can you tell me about children in Victorian London? The ones who didn't come from well-off families?"

Marie puts her hand up and Mrs Emery nods. "I'll let you do hands up for now, Marie, but later I'm going to ask people randomly so everyone gets a chance to say something." She looks at her pot of lolly sticks. "What can you tell me?"

"They were made to work at a young age. And lots of them couldn't read. Some kids wanted more than they had and worked together and found a way to get it," she says. "Sometimes there were child gangs. They had their own rules and their own codes of what was right or wrong, and none of the adults could do anything about it." She seems very pleased with herself, and she turns, then, to look at me. And winks. Actually winks.

I blink back. I've never winked in my life, never had a reason to wink, or be winked at, and I can't think of a reason to wink now either. What did she mean by it? I think of the ketchup from lunch, so casually pulled from her pocket, and how none of them said anything about it, even though they could have got into trouble. The After School

Crime Club. What a name!

"Great!" says Mrs Emery, tapping the excerpt of text in front of her. "Remember we have to use evidence to back up our opinions. Can you give me some evidence from the text to back it up?"

"Hmmm," says Marie, looking down at the text and picking up a green highlighter, making a display of highlighting something on the page. "Well, it says they had to find ways to keep warm, and eat, but also they were still children who wanted to have fun."

"Wonderful!" says Mrs Emery.

I wonder what it would be like to be in a world where adults don't tell you what to do. Would I like it? Do I trust Mum to tell me what to do for the best, the best for me, when she imagines me owning and running my own chain of cinemas, when what I'd really like to do is just work in a cinema and spend my time outside work watching old movies and maybe doing a blog or something about why more people should watch them?

Who'd read a blog you'd write? a voice in my head says. I don't know whose it is, but it seems very certain. *You can barely spell.*

This annoys me. And I look up at Marie again.

She is looking at me. She has written something on her whiteboard and is holding it up for me to read.

WHO NEEDS ADULTS ANYWAY??

This makes me grin and before I know what I'm doing, I pull out my whiteboard and pen and write.

NOT ME!!!

Marie giggles and nods. Then she writes something else, gets up to pretend to put something in the bin when Mrs Emery has her back turned, and then pops her whiteboard down on the desk in front of me. YOUR NEXT DARE IS TO TAKE SOMETHING FROM THE BOOK BOX. WE'LL GIVE IT TO A CHARITY SHOP AFTER SO IT'S NOT REALLY STEALING.

And suddenly, I'm both dreading and completely excited for After School (Crime) Club.

CHAPTER 8

Rich is dropping me off at The Book Box. He picks me up from school wearing his jeans and T-shirt and trainers combo, as predicted, and when I hop in he says, "How's your mum been, Will?"

I think about how to answer this but before I do, he says, "Sorry. I mean how was your day?"

"It was different," I say. "I ate lunch with some of the others who go to After School Club."

"And that's ... good different?" he says, pulling out into traffic.

"I think so," I say. "Marie's been in my class since we were in Reception, and she's never spoken to me before. Other than when she was an angel in the nativity and I was a sheep and she said, 'Please move, dear sheep, so that I can see the baby Jesus.' I only just remembered that."

Rich laughs. "A great line."

"I think she ad libbed it," I say. "I don't think she was supposed to ask me to move out of the way."

"At least she wasn't Mary," he says.

I laugh. "She's been nice to me today." I leave out what she said about doing stuff without adults knowing about it. I definitely leave out the bit about giving her the otter he brought Mum back from the Isle of Skye. And I can hardly think straight about the dare. To take something from the shop? That is definitely stealing. But then … we'd give it to a charity shop? So we wouldn't keep it. And a charity would benefit. Maybe they'd let me give it to the Age UK shop like Nanna's things. Is that bad? Is right and wrong as simple as all that?

I don't know.

Trusting my gut like Nanna always said to is harder than I thought when I feel this confused and … excited?

Rich might understand, or at least talk kindly to me about it, but I need to think it through for myself first. I may not have friends, but I'm not stupid. I know there is a difference between doing things behind adults' backs, doing things adults think are bad for you, and breaking the law.

"That's nice. There might be some good things about going that you weren't expecting."

"There might," I agree. "But don't tell Mum."

"She wants the best for you and loves you."

"I know."

"So how's she been?" He says it again so casually, like it doesn't come with the weight of all that's happened over the past few months. He's only been away for two weeks, and in that time the house got pretty bad, but she *has* sorted it now, like she always does. I like that he looks out for her. I like that he notices things, even though she does her best to make sure he doesn't.

"She's been all right," I say. "She's been very busy. She won't come with me to see Nanna's grave. She was taking Nanna's things to the Age UK shop and didn't seem very sad about it."

"That's understandable, don't you think? You know your mum. She keeps busy to keep her mind off things," he says. "She just needs time."

"We only have one life," I say. "In this body at least. We only get a certain amount of time."

"She's been through a lot," he says.

"I know," I say, and manage not to add, *And so have I*. I wonder if they have conversations like this about me.

"Have you been to Nanna's grave?" he says then, and I shake my head.

"I still go to her house though," I say. "And I've looked over the hedge into the cemetery, once." I don't say anything about the key. Or Tay. I think he probably knows about the key already. I hope he doesn't know about the otter. I glance at him, but he seems quite calm.

He pulls up on the double yellow lines and I hop out. I say thank you and he says any time and have a good time and I say I will and he says he'll pick me up after and maybe we can go for a drive-through. I say yes please, because I'll need something greasy and disgusting after the healthy brain food I'll be subjected to at Club.

The bell over the door rings as I push it open and I'm the first one there from my school. Nish, Jamie and Pav are there, with their smarter uniforms, Pav with his tie around his wrist, and they're already looking at a worksheet, sitting together this time around one table. I know why the others aren't there yet. They walk together from school. At the end of the day, Marie said, "After you complete the next dare, maybe you'd like to walk to Club with us?" I said I'd have to ask my mum, and Dan smirked. Brynn was walking ahead of them, with headphones on. He didn't say anything or even acknowledge them, or me.

I would like to walk with them. Anything to prove to Tay that I don't care about rules. That I'm *interesting*. If Marie accepts me, then maybe Tay will.

There's been no sign of Tay so far. At school or after.

"Willow!" says Jed enthusiastically, getting my name right this time.

"Hi, Jed," I say. "Hi, Rox."

"Hi, Willow! Lovely to see you. Glad we didn't frighten you away."

Once again, nobody else laughs. It's impressive how enthusiastic Jed and Rox are in the face of so little positive feedback.

"Still here," I say, and shrug. I take a seat, and a cookie which I'll let Tay have if she wants it. I pour some water from the jug. None of it feels so threatening this time. I feel all right. Although my heart is beating fast about the next dare. And that word. CRIME.

"Just some quiet work to get on with today," says Rox. "No discussions. Just see what you can do on this."

I look at the piece of paper and it's practice SATs questions. A reading paper. Urgh. Why do they want to know what I understand from reading these things? Don't they know already? Don't they get bored reading all the answers of all the kids all over the country writing slightly different versions of the same thing?

I read the first piece of text. It's a poem about sheep but I guess it's a poem about something else because poems are always about something else.

Sheep in the field. The sun
A coin at market. Grass
Not green, but brown, a thick mud-crust.

I stop reading. It reminds me of the gravy on the left-out washing up that there'll be no sign of while Rich is here. Luckily, I'm saved from the symbolism of sheep by the bell going and Brynn walking in, still with his headphones on, followed by Marie and Dan. They all nod hello, and the three of them take the seats in a row to my left, the gang back together, whatever their falling out was, forgiven. The other seat next to me is still free, the one Tay sat in last time. Phew.

We all sit and do our work quietly. The poem isn't too bad. A load of stuff about whether eating animals is part of nature's cycle or not and whether we can own animals. I don't think we can really own animals. Can we really own anything? This makes me think of the dare. Is it really stealing when you're taking a thing from one place and putting it in another, and not getting anything for it or actually using it? I write in full sentences and use evidence from the text. I'll probably get zero marks. I always miss the point.

"When Tay comes in," whispers Marie, "I bet she won't sit with us."

I forget to hide my disappointment. "Why not?"

"She wants to know if you're one of us or not," says Dan.

"What does that mean?" I feel like I'm losing my patience with all this code talk. Even though I love old musicals, I never like the farce stuff much – the bit where characters are confused and make mistakes and the audience laughs at them. I mean, I like watching it, but I don't like being part of it.

"It means, like I said earlier, there are some tests to pass before we let you in on the big stuff. The reason we started The After School Crime Club was because some things are just unfair. Why should some kids have so much stuff and others have nothing? Just because some families have more money?"

That is actually a good point. Nanna always

said to trust your instincts, your gut reaction, because that's the part of you that knows things in the moment, and it's always right.

"Are you ... like Robin Hood?" I say suddenly, then feel embarrassed.

"Ha! Yes!" says Marie without flinching. "Told you she'd get it," she says to Dan, and Brynn looks at me. He shakes his head.

And then Tay comes in. She does it quietly, without show or comment, although she still has her huge bag over her shoulder, and wears her uniform like she's her own personal stylist. I look up at her and smile and pull out the chair for her to sit in, and I nod at the cookie to show her I've saved it for her. And for a moment she pauses. She looks at me. Then she looks at Marie, and at Dan, then Brynn. And ... she walks right past. She walks right past and takes a chair at the already crowded table with the kids from the other school, leaving me, Marie, Dan and Brynn on our own. An island. I fight back tears. I feel shocked. I knew I wasn't cool enough to be friends with Tay Welding. Unless I do something about it, I'll always be a bit too *weird*.

It's all very well Nanna saying be yourself. But

what if yourself isn't good enough? Mum's always saying it. My grades are always saying it. The very fact I'm here in this room says it. I feel sick. I think I'm going to be sick. I sit and do the rest of my paper in silence. I ignore everyone. I write my answers to the "reading a recipe" question. (150g sugar is the answer to question *a*. Even I know that.)

I stay in my cocoon just hoping it will soon be over. Sometimes I look up and think, what could I take from this shop that wouldn't be too expensive, and wouldn't cause a big problem for Jed and Rox, and wouldn't really be stealing?

These are not easy questions to answer.

A lot of time must have passed because somehow it's the end of the session and I've said nothing to anybody, and nobody's said anything to me.

"Great!" says Rox, cutting through the silence. "That's enough for today."

With that, Tay gets up and walks out.

Not even a goodbye. Not one look or smile or anything. I feel sick. I feel like I've got something terribly wrong and there's no way to fix it. Why does this matter so much to me? Other kids have never mattered to me before. Why now?

"Right," says Marie brightly, and I hope she can't see the tears welling up in my eyes. "So…"

I don't want Tay Welding to ignore me and pretend like I don't exist ever again. Just for the chance to have another conversation with her, I'd probably do anything.

But then Marie says, "So…" again and I say, "I'm in." Just like that.

"Great," says Dan. "Take it. Take it right out of the shop and take it home with you. Tay wants to know you're serious about not caring about the rules. At the minute she's not sure. She thinks you might be … too *good* to be one of us."

First I'm too weird. Then I'm too good. I don't know what to say. It's one of those moments in life when you can go in one of two directions. I've had them before, but not like this. I've never stolen anything in my life. I've never wanted anything enough to steal it. I've never even thought about stealing something. Once, the man in the corner shop gave me too much change when I went to buy washing up liquid and some air freshener to kickstart Mum, and I took it back. Not because *I* didn't want to get in trouble, but because

I worried *he'd* get in trouble at the end of the day when they counted up all the money. I kept it in my pocket for half an hour, considered keeping the extra £2 coin. But I couldn't do it. I wouldn't have been able to enjoy it. So I took it back.

But here I am. Not saying no. Considering it. Looking around the shop for books I could take. Thinking... Could I? Just this once? Just a book. Nobody would notice. They've got a ton of them... We'd be giving it to charity...

"I've said I'm in." I hear the words coming out of my mouth. I feel sweaty, like hot water is falling from my face on to the table, like my body is a tap. I can hear my heartbeat louder than the other kids' voices, louder than the classical music Jed has put on in the background, louder than anything I've ever heard in my life. Louder even than the MGM opening fanfare. All I can hear is my heart and the words, *Just this once, just this once, just this once. Why do you always have to be so good? Why do you always do what you're told? Who needs adults anyway...?*

"Great!" say Marie, Dan and Brynn at the same time.

"I told Tay you'd do it. She didn't believe me.

Said you're too soft. You have to give it to her tomorrow. At school. Whatever it is you take, you have to give it to her, to prove you did it. It can't be a rubber or a pen or something. It has to cost … over fifteen pounds. That's the challenge. Then she'll give it to charity."

That hurts. I'm not soft. I'm the opposite of soft. I've never once cried about Dad leaving. I never once cried about Nanna dying either. That's not me. I'll show them. I'll show Tay Welding, and then she'll sit next to me and tell me about cricket, and say she likes my name, and I'll know I'm good enough, and maybe, I think, ridiculously – I know it's ridiculous even as I think it – she'll come with me to see *High Society* at the Arts Centre and we will become *friends*.

"Can we take it to the Age UK shop?" I say suddenly. "It's where Mum's taking my late Nanna's things."

The three of them look at me and say nothing. Until Marie smiles brightly. "The Age UK Shop. Of course we can! What a lovely idea!" And that makes me feel a bit better.

So, I do it. I do the dare.

And it's so easy.

I walk over to thank Jed and Rox for the session. I say I think I'm starting to understand my work better. I say I didn't really want to come but my mum made me and I'm glad she did. They are smiling, feeling proud of themselves, feeling like they have made a difference. You can tell by their faces. And while they smile, while they are feeling happy, I slide a big thick book called *101 Facts About Cricket* that's right there on the "Sports" shelf beside them into my open school bag. I hold my folded coat over it and pull it to my chest and for a moment I think, *They must have seen me, they must have.* Then I think, *Is this worth over fifteen pounds?* But it's too late to check now.

"I'm really glad to hear that," says Jed, and I feel the raspberry-jam colour spread up my chest.

"Same time on Friday?"

"Absolutely!" I say as though I haven't just done what I've done. What else do The After School Crime Club do? *What else are they going to get you to do?* I shake off that thought. And the other one: *You don't think this is the last thing they'll ask from you, do you? You're not that stupid?*

I just have to get out of the shop with the book. Just that. I feel like surely everyone can see what

I've done, surely they're going to stop me on my way out, shouting "Stop! Thief!" But. Nothing happens. I step out into the cold air and nothing happens. I don't even look to see if Marie, Dan and Brynn saw me do it. Nobody is there. All that happens is Rich pulls up and gives me a little wave, and I jump into his navy Mazda.

"All good?" he says kindly, so kindly I could confess everything right then and beg for forgiveness. But I don't. I look out of the window and see Marie, Brynn and Dan now out on the street, waving at me. They look so pleased, so impressed. So I wave back.

"Yes. All good," I say as my heartbeat begins to slow and I realise I've got away with it. "We still having a drive-through?" I suddenly feel really hungry. The cookie I'd saved for Tay is still sitting on the plate inside The Book Box and I haven't eaten anything since lunch.

"Great," says Rich, and I think, *Can you see? Can you see I'm different? Can you see what I've done?* But he chatters on about otters, and the Isle of Skye, and about when his new job starts in Hexham. And I'm right here, in my seat, tightly held by my seatbelt, with my secret.

CHAPTER 9

So it turns out I can steal things.

Things that cost £19.99, in fact. More than what they asked me for.

I wasn't expecting to be able to do that.

It doesn't matter that I could barely sleep last night, or that when I did I had a dream about Nanna shaking her head at me as I walked through her garden on all fours, snuffling, twenty-pound notes stuck all over my body like hedgehog spines.

Or that part of me knows it was wrong.

Don't forget, I tell myself. *They are giving it to charity. Nobody's going to be keeping it. Any money it's sold for will help someone.*

Maybe I'm weird *and* interesting?

I walk into school with my head high. I don't feel bad. I don't. They thought I couldn't do it. Tay Welding thought I couldn't do it, but Marie stood up for me and knew I could. And I proved Tay wrong and Marie right. I'm ready for any of the things they throw at me. It's not even about making friends any more. It's about … proving I'm not what everyone thinks I am. And I sort of feel on a high. Like I'm the one in the spotlight instead of the one behind the camera. Like I have my own theme song. That people are dancing around me, not in front of me.

I've never cared what other people think about me before. Nanna's always been there to say I'm OK as I am, and I've always believed her.

But Nanna's not here any more.

And things are changing.

Soon Rich will live with us, and next year I'll be in high school. Mum's always talking about the future. Maybe it's time to plan my own.

The classroom looks different. Smaller. For the first time I notice more about the other children. The pencil cases. The hairstyles. The collars on the school T-shirts – some folded properly, some creased, some tucked under their jumpers, some bright white and wafting the smell of fabric softener, others grey from a mixed wash and as crumpled as frowns.

I notice the shoebox on Mrs Emery's desk with the slot cut in the top and the bright writing on the side: "The Big Walk: Sponsorship Money". A lot of kids in the class have taken part in The Big Walk on the weekends. People gave them money to go for long walks with their families. It's for a local charity. I was going to speak to Mum about doing it together. But. A good moment never arrived. And now it's too late and the school are just collecting all the money everyone else managed to raise.

What have I been doing all this time, sitting in my own bubble, not really noticing anything? There is a spare seat on Marie's table and as I walk in she says, "Willow! Willow! I asked Mrs Emery if you could sit here and she said yes!" She looks so happy about it, how can I say no?

I sit down without thinking, get out my pencil case and my bottle of water. Marie is smiling at me. "Dad says do you want to come over after school?" she says. "One day soon?" and I think, wow, somebody has asked me over after school. I'm sure I can miss seeing Nanna one time. Maybe it will encourage Mum to go.

"I'd like that," I say. And out of nowhere, I add, "And maybe you could come round mine."

"I'd LOVE that," says Marie. "We can watch a movie and eat popcorn!"

Marie likes movies. "Yes!" I say. "Yes, please." Always be polite, that's what Nanna said. But I doubt Marie will want to watch an old movie. You never know, though. I'm feeling brave.

"I like old movies," I say. "Do you?"

"Oh yes!" says Marie. "My dad got me into *Back to the Future* and *Indiana Jones* and all those ones from the 1980s. I love them!"

I don't tell her that's not what I mean by old. She looks different today. Her hair isn't as neat as usual. It's pulled up into a lumpy ponytail when usually it's plaited. "You've done something different with your hair," I say.

She shoots me a look. "It looks nice," I add quickly.

"Ah, thanks." She softens. "Dad did it. Usually my neighbour does it. She's our childminder. She used to be Tay's childminder too, though Tay doesn't go any more. I'll be too old for a childminder soon, so I'm practising doing plaits on myself."

"It looks nice," I repeat. I decide not to ask where her mum is. And, for now, I decide not to ask why Tay doesn't go to the childminder any more. If she wanted to tell me, she would.

"Great!" I say. I have a tight feeling in my chest, so it's good timing that Mrs Emery shushes everybody for the register then we get on with arithmetic practice.

122×24=
166×53=
189×88=

I hate my eight times table. I can never remember it. I've said it out loud, I've repeated it so many times, I even tried learning it with Nanna. Rich helped once. I just can't remember past 3x8. There are gaps where the numbers should be. Long multiplication is the worst. I know you have to carry the extra zero because you are multiplying tens on the second line, but I often forget, or I do it the wrong way round and multiply the tens before I multiply the ones. I could use place value, but that's a lot of counters to draw, and I just don't see numbers that way. Sometimes it feels like I don't *see* numbers at all.

"Stuck?" says Marie. Her page is full of workings out, and when I try to read them, it all looks like nonsense.

"A bit," I say.

"Well, it doesn't matter," says Marie. "I'm awful at English, and you're good at that, aren't you?"

Am I? I don't know. I like it better than maths though.

She gets out her whiteboard and writes in really

small letters: *Did you do it?* Then when she's sure I've read it, she wipes it out with the back of her hand.

I nod.

Next, she writes: *You've got to give it to Tay today*, and my eyes widen. I hadn't thought about how the book was going to get to Tay. I certainly hadn't pictured me giving it to her. At school.

I write: *Do I have to?*

And Marie nods, seriously.

When?

Marie nods at the window. Then writes: *When you see her go past the window to the toilets. She always goes just before lunch. Ask to go to the toilet and take it to her. Right?*

Mrs Emery comes over and Marie writes a quick calculation on the whiteboard. "...And then you carry the two, does that make sense?" And I can't help but admire her speed and her look of total innocence.

"That makes sense," I say, nodding. Mrs Emery looks pleased. "How lovely, Marie, that you're helping Willow. Remember not to give her the answers, just prompts. I think this seating arrangement is going to work really well."

"So do I!" says Marie cheerfully. "And I won't let Willow cheat. I promise!"

"I wouldn't cheat," I say quickly. I hate cheating. I'd rather lose a game, get a question wrong, get anything wrong, rather than cheat. Cheating means you get something you don't deserve, or get praise for something you don't deserve praise for. My stomach hurts. Stealing is cheating in a way, isn't it? And aren't I a thief now?

"Ahhh, everyone cheats sometimes, don't they?" says Marie as Mrs Emery walks away. "It's fun!"

But that sounds wrong to me. I look up at the window to see if Tay is there. How on earth am I going to give her the book? Last night at Club, she didn't even look at me. My heart beats hard in my chest again. It's becoming a regular thing. I wonder if I should ask Mum to take me to the doctor?

High Society was Grace Kelly's last film. She died when she was 52. I wonder what it was like, to star in films where you were made up to look like the most beautiful person on earth. I wonder if she'd have liked to play an ugly character. One who gets things wrong. One who looks a bit scruffy. One whose favourite sweater is the green one with a burger in sunglasses on it, and who has never worn a dress since she was a toddler. One who likes lying on her front on her bed looking through old film scripts, listening to old movie scores, working out how the director got the actors to do this, or that. How much was choreographed, and how much was just there, in the moment, because of the actors and the trick of the light, or just ... by magic?

I doubt it.

What did Nanna say? *It takes all sorts.* That's always made me feel better. There's no one way to be a person. She used to say it to explain Mum. Mum is a person who on the outside is always so neat, so well put together, but who behind closed doors... What? Struggles? I've tried not to think about the in-between times, when Mum can't seem to sort out the laundry or the washing up ... or anything. When the letters pile up on the counter. When she stares out of the window, just stares, with the radio on, and I help myself to whatever I want from the fridge, and put myself to bed, wondering if it will be different tomorrow.

When it is different, it's like that version of Mum

never existed, and I wonder, sometimes, if I've imagined it. I wonder if Mum is OK. I wonder – I try to push that thought away – if *I'm* OK.

I've been daydreaming for ages, not talking, just staring at my work. We've moved on to English and Topic (World War Two. Evacuees. What it would be like to leave your family and be with a totally different one when there was no Internet, no email, no mobile phones). It comes as a surprise when Marie elbows me in the ribs and goes, "Look! Now's your chance!"

I see Tay go past the window, walking in that slouchy but confident way she does. *I can't do this*, I think. *I can't do this*. But another part of me puts my hand up and says, "Can I go to the toilet, please, Mrs Emery?" hoping she'll say no and that will be that, but instead she says, "Of course you can, Willow. Remember to wash your hands." Mrs Emery has a thing about reminding us to wash our hands. I always do.

The walk to the toilets takes three hundred and seventy-five years.

When I open the door, Tay is right there, standing in front of the mirror, smoothing her hair back into that neat quiff, looking at herself, with no expression on her face. Her big bag isn't with her. I wonder if she uses it to carry all the things she steals. I wonder what other things she steals. Am I allowed to just talk about what happened yesterday? Do I just give her the book? I'm not sure of the rules and I don't want to get it wrong.

"Hi," I say, feeling brave. "How are you?"

Tay shrugs and catches my eye in the mirror, and looks away and smiles. "Is this going to be weird, or interesting?"

I smile too. I am already feeling like what I'm about to give her will prove I'm definitely on the interesting side of that equation.

"Interesting," I say confidently. "I've got something for you," I say, thinking how weird this is, that we both know what I've got for her, and we both know why, but I'm standing here pretending like I don't, and so is Tay, as she hardly looks interested, or even like she cares if I stole the book or not.

"Oh yeah?" Tay turns around and looks at me, properly looks at me, and I want to say, *See? You underestimated me!* But I don't. I just reach into my school bag and pull out the book and hold it out to her. The shiny foil lettering of the title catches the orange lights of the toilets, and for a moment I'm blinded. A flash, like someone's taken a photograph.

"This," I say, and Tay holds out her hand and takes it, frowns a little, looks confused, and then pleased.

"Cricket!" she says.

"Yes. You like cricket," I say. "I remember you said."

"And your name's Willow." She smiles. "Like the bat."

"Like the bat."

We stand there, both of us still holding the book. Both of us awkward, almost. I expected her to be harder. To be like, "Well, you've passed the test. Now you're one of us." But she says, "That's really thoughtful, thank you."

And this confuses me. I nearly say, "You told me to do it," but I don't.

"I hope you're pleased," I say.

"I am," says Tay. "I haven't got this one." I let go and she holds it to her like Mum held Rich to her when he gave her the flowers and the wine and the otter, and for a moment she seems really young, younger than she is, younger than the mini adult she often seems to be, younger than those Year 3 and 4 kids who used to crowd around my table at lunch before Marie, Dan and Brynn arrived.

"So, you like cricket?" says Tay, looking like herself again, holding tightly on to the book.

"I do," I lie. It's a small lie. I can learn to like cricket.

"What else do you like?" Tay stands with one hand in her pocket and the other around the book. This moment makes it worth it. She is talking to me. Really talking to me. Saying more than she ever would have had I not taken the book. What is a book worth anyway? This one cost £19.99 and it's going to go to Age UK and make some money for someone who doesn't have much. Like Nanna's things Mum keeps taking, box by box.

I'm about to answer her. It feels like everything is going to come tumbling out. Old movies, how I keep singing "Singin' in the Rain" since I first sat next to her, *High Society* at the Arts Centre, Mum, Dad, Nanna, Rich, the rug in my room that's shaped like a director's clapper board. The smell of honeysuckle in Nanna's garden. How I like plain cheese sandwiches. All of it.

But, instead, the bell goes.

"Lunch," we both say, and laugh.

"Are you going to sit with me, Marie, Dan and Brynn?" I say suddenly. I'm still feeling brave. I feel like I can do anything or be anything and have anything I want. I feel like something's shifted in me and nothing will be the same again.

Tay frowns, the moment broken, and walks towards the toilet door.

"Nah," she says. "And, to be clear, that's a *big* nah." She carries the "ahhh" sound on for ages, like she's singing. I feel myself crumple. It stings. All that gentleness from a minute ago is gone. I can't see a sign of anything in her eyes. They are a dark cloud and she's still frowning. "The *biggest*," she adds, unnecessarily in my opinion, and then she turns round and swings out of the door, so that it's just me, with my empty hands, and my confused feelings. What did I do wrong? I've done everything they've asked of me, and it's still not enough.

This is why I've never had friends. This is why I've never wanted them.

She's taken the book though. She hasn't left it.

Marie suddenly appears next to me, as I stand

there like I've been slapped. "You did it?"

"I did." I feel flat. Like a party balloon long after a party. Not that I've ever had a party.

"What did she say?" Marie's eyes are bright. Her ponytail is swinging about and she is almost jumping with excitement.

"She said thank you," I say. "And she seemed pleased…"

"That's great. I knew you could do it!"

"But then she was… She…"

"She was mean?"

"Yes."

"Ah, that's her way. She's pleased you passed the test."

"She is?"

"Yes."

I feel a bit better.

"And now you're ready for the next one."

"The next one…" I deflate some more. I knew there'd be more. I knew it when I said yes to the first one. When I took the book. When I sat in the car with Rich and felt the heat of it in my bag on my lap, Gene Kelly tutting at me with disapproval from his silver frame.

"The next one!" says Marie, like it's something

to look forward to.

"Which is…"

And then Marie takes my arm, squeezes it and says something that fills me with genuine dread. The words fall like hot marbles into my stomach. I can feel them rattling there, rolling into each other, tap tap tap.

"Tell me about your stepdad."

"My… What?"

"Richard Cherni, isn't it?"

Hearing Rich's name like that, out of Marie's mouth, makes me feel sick. I've barely mentioned him, just once when I gave her the otter. I've certainly never called him my stepdad or said his surname. I'm confused and I don't even try hiding it.

"What about him? Why are you asking about him?"

"He sells jewellery, right?" I look at the charm bracelet Marie made herself, dangling prettily from her wrist.

"He doesn't sell them exactly…"

"He has access to nice jewellery?"

And then I get it. Marie is telling me Tay Welding wants me to steal some jewellery from

Rich. That's what I have to do to prove myself and be part of their group.

I won't do it. I *won't*.

Rich doesn't deserve it. I like him.

But someone else talks out of my mouth instead of me, and I hear a voice that's familiar, just like mine, saying something I'd never, ever say.

"OK," I say. "When?"

"As soon as possible!" says Marie quickly. "We'll give it to a charity shop again, obviously. Or take it to a shop that buys second-hand jewellery and give the money to charity – maybe keep a little for ourselves to celebrate. A little party! Once you've taken the jewellery, you're a member. Then we can move on to the good stuff. The *team* stuff."

The word "team" hangs in the air. So does the word "party".

"In fact, you could do it tonight!" says Marie. "And then come over to mine before school tomorrow and we could walk together!" She squeezes my arm.

I nod. I have no idea what Mum would say about me going to a friend's house, for the first time, with no prior warning. I think of her looking at photos of people she knows online, and the photos of their children with their friends. She'd love it. I know she would. I'd love it. Walking into school with someone else.

"OK…" I say slowly. "And we're giving the jewellery to Age UK?"

Marie laughs and shakes her head. "Actually, we can't just take a piece of jewellery to Age UK," she says, as though that should be obvious. "But Dan knows someone who can sell it, and we can…" She ponders for a moment. "We can take the money to one of those donation boxes." She looks at me, but I show no reaction. I'm thinking about how we'd even do that. I'm thinking of how I'd even get access to Rich's jewellery. I'm thinking, *If I do this, I really am a thief*. But it's like I'm in a cart hurtling down a hill and there's no way to get out until I crash into something at the bottom.

"Like Robin Hood!" says Marie enthusiastically. "I bet the jewellery's all insured anyway, right? They'll just replace it and it's a victimless crime. You think Rich would suspect you?"

"No…" I say, which makes it feel worse somehow.

"Come on!" says Marie. "It will be fun! No rules, remember!"

In *High Society* there's a song with the line, "What a swell party, a swell party, a swellegant, elegant party this is!" For a moment I see myself at a party like that. Tay and me singing, dressed like Bing Crosby and Frank Sinatra. It's not really stealing if it's samples, is it? If we're giving the money to charity? And Rich is insured?

I mean. It is stealing. But. It's not fair that some people can afford stuff like that, and some can't. I'll be like Robin Hood. And we'll celebrate!

So, it's decided. I've decided.

And then we go to lunch.

CHAPTER 10

For the first time in my life, I walk home with other kids, and not by myself. There's no After School (Crime) Club, but four of the main members, everyone but Tay, are here and we walk along the embankment from school. Me, Marie, Dan and Brynn. Brynn's got his headphones in, but it doesn't matter really. Maybe he's jealous about their group of three becoming a four. Maybe he just doesn't like me.

I feel excited. Nervous. Sick.

I am interesting, I am not weird.

I realise that at eleven years old I've never walked home with anyone but Mum. I've never been part of those laughing groups, tugging at bags, pushing each other into the road, chirruping like birds. Or squawking. Marie walks in the middle, linking arms with me and Dan. She's super excited, keeps talking about when I'm going to go over to hers for tea tomorrow, and I can't help but get caught up in it.

I just have to steal the jewellery tonight. Just one piece. It doesn't have to be hugely fancy. I can do this.

I'm hoping they'll forget about all the stealing stuff once they trust me, hoping Tay won't have any bigger plans for me. *Do you even want to be friends with someone like Tay Welding?* says a voice in my head that sounds very much like Nanna. But I don't listen. *Never judge a movie by its poster*, her voice says instead. And that sounds better.

And it's weird. When Tay and I are alone, she seems … kind. Funny. And like she likes me.

"We were thinking of getting the train to Oxford on the weekend," says Dan quietly. "Do you want to come?"

"By yourselves?" I say. I've never been on public transport without an adult, although I've walked to plenty of places by myself.

"Yeah," says Dan. "We do it all the time."

"I'll have to ask Mum," I say. I can't imagine that she'll say yes but she also wants me to have friends, so if I word it the right way, and catch her at the right moment, who knows?

"Maybe…" I say. "Will Tay be coming?"

They both snigger, and I feel embarrassed.

"No way," says Dan. "She doesn't like trains."

"She doesn't like people," adds Marie. "Unless they *prove* themselves, obviously," she adds quickly. Something about the way Marie says this makes me feel sick. I am tired of trying to prove myself. I don't want to prove myself. In that moment, with the cars driving past, with the sound of other kids, and the streetlights overhead, I want to say "I'm through with proving myself, actually."

But, of course, I don't say that.

Dan pops into the newsagents just up from The Book Box and comes out with pockets full of sweets for us to share.

"How much did all that cost?" I say. I've never seen so many snacks in one person's pockets.

"How much do you think?" says Dan, laughing.

"Don't you get it, Willow?" says Marie, as though I am much younger than her, not three months older than her like I actually am.

"Of course I do," I say defensively. "I get everything."

"Then you'll know," says Marie in a voice I don't much like, "that we never pay for anything if we don't have to. Right, Dan?"

Dan nods. "Why should anyone pay for something other people have easily? Money makes no sense."

I can't argue with that. Nanna always talked

about how money is luck and your worth is not tied up with your job title, or your bank balance, or your family history or anything. Why should some people have more just because they were born with more? Mum and Nanna disagreed about that. Mum talks about aspiration. Nanna talked about inspiration. They argued about politics a lot and when anything came on the TV about it, Mum always turned it off while Nanna said, "There's nothing wrong with a good debate if you're willing to listen." "Since when did you listen?" Mum replied. And so it went on.

I'm pretty sure they'd both think your friends stealing from the shop whenever they want is wrong though, says another voice. But, to be honest, I'm getting tired of all the voices and all I want to do is work out which one is mine.

But this is definitely stealing for themselves and not to help anyone else. If this was a musical a spotlight would come on me, and there'd be a big drum, getting faster, to show the speed of my heartbeat.

Are you really going to do this? Yes I am.

I need Tay to see me differently. I need her to take me seriously.

The afternoon light is like raspberry ripple ice cream. It's one of those skies where, if it was the backdrop to a scene, it would be for the moment the couple kiss, or the friends are reunited, or something good is about to happen. It's beautiful, and the line of trees that stretch over the path towards Nanna's are arms above my head. Reaching out to each other. Telling each other secrets.

I wish they'd tell me what to do.

I'll do chores to make up for stealing the jewellery. I'll be good and helpful and not argue with Mum ever again. That will make Rich happy. Yes. That's what I'll do. Doing this dare will make home life better. Because I'll feel so guilty I'll do anything to make it up to Rich. And Mum. And Nanna.

This thought is comforting. Almost.

I eat the Mars bar Dan has given me as we say our goodbyes at the top of my street.

"I can't wait to see you tomorrow!" says Marie. "I know you can do it!"

"Good luck, mate," says Dan. "Next dare is one we'll do all together!"

Brynn looks at me, then at Marie. He says,

"Take care of yourself, Willow," and sounds, once again, like a grown-up.

I walk away and don't look back, and before I know it I'm home, inside the kitchen, where Rich is working at the table because Tuesdays are his day for catching up on paperwork, and he's promised to order in pizza. I look at him and think, *Can I really do this?*

"Hi, Will!" he says cheerily. My heart is a drum. It's a whole percussion section. An orchestra.

"Hi, Rich!" I say. *It's not too late to not do this.*

But. I'm too far in to say no. I don't know how I'd get out of it tomorrow morning. Marie is expecting me at her place to give her whatever it is I steal from him, and I can't just turn up empty handed.

"Would you like a cup of tea?" I say brightly. It's horrible. This act. But I push on through, thinking of my happy ending.

"Oh, yes, please. How was your day?"

I stride about, making the tea, and tell him. Sort of. "I walked home with some of the others from Club," I say. "It was fun. And Marie, you know the one who told me to move out of the way when I was a sheep... Well, she asked me to go over to hers and walk with her to school tomorrow. I said yes. Do you think Mum will be all right with it?"

He does a little punch to the air to celebrate my success. "Too right she will!" he smiles. "That's brilliant."

It would really help me right now if Rich said something unkind or unfair, just to make what's about to happen easier. But he doesn't. So I have to push on regardless.

"We're doing a project at school!" I blurt out. "Designing our own jewellery. Do you think you could show me your samples? For inspiration?"

I place the tea down on a coaster. Mum's bought new coasters to go with the new everything. Rich looks delighted.

"At last! The girl who doesn't like jewellery has a use for my jewellery!" He leaps up. If only he knew. I try to look innocent even though I know that I am not. I am a thief. I am a member of The After School Crime Club. I can trick someone who likes me into letting me take something from them. Urgh.

He gets the briefcase with the code combination lock from the cupboard under the stairs and opens it quickly on the table, pushing his laptop aside and talking quickly.

"So these are actually mock-ups of the really expensive stuff," he explains. "I don't carry the stuff worth thousands around with me. But this is still good costume jewellery. Still looks the part. Worth a few quid."

My heart sinks. Does Marie know that the jewellery Rich takes around with him isn't the proper stuff? I didn't. I'd seen the brochures with the real prices. £1,200. £3,000. £10,000. It had never crossed my mind that the jewellery he had with him wasn't worth that much.

"How much are these ones worth?" I say as casually as I can, as he brings out bracelets and necklaces, all shimmering in the kitchen lights, all sparkly, and silver and gold.

"Oh, they're still worth a few quid." He holds up a necklace that has a pretty gold chain and a gold pendant with a little gemstone star sparkling in the middle. "One hundred for this one, even though it's a fake. We don't sell these ones though."

It's perfect for the job. And they don't even sell them. It reminds me of Marie's homemade clay bracelet, and I think she'll like this one. So

I pretend to listen to him talking about settings and clasps and a bezel on a watch that if it was the real version would cost nearly £10,000, but all the while I watch the necklace and wait for my moment.

I keep him talking until Mum comes in.

I haven't thought about how he'll know it was me when he finds it missing.

I haven't thought about how I'll explain it's missing.

I know he'll believe me if I say I didn't do it, and that makes the whole thing worse somehow. But it also makes it easier.

Mum says, "Oh! How nice. You want to see the jewellery!" And she joins us at the table, holding things up to the light, being very careful, saying "ooh" at all the right moments. Rich looks happy. Mum looks happy. I look at the necklace.

"Are we still having pizza?" I say quickly. "Can I have plain cheese?"

"Of course we are, and of course you can," says Rich, picking up his phone.

"Shall me and Mum put the jewellery away?" I say quickly.

"Ahhh," says Mum. "Do you remember when

you used to play with my jewellery box when you were little? You used to love putting everything back into the right slots. You used to want to wear it then."

"I remember," I say. It seems a long time ago. I used to walk in front of Dad and twirl around wearing it all. It may as well be a million years ago.

It's funny. The more I've been hanging out with Marie, the less I hear Nanna's voice. Is that because I'm finally starting to see that she's not here any more? Finally starting to learn to do things on my own?

I hear her then. *This is more like* Singin' in the Rain *than you think, Willow. You are Lina, with someone else's voice coming out of your mouth. But it's not someone nice who can sing, like Debbie Reynolds. It's Marie. And the words that come out of your mouth aren't lovely songs. They're something else.*

Argh. *Not now, Nanna.* I need to do this.

So.

While Rich is tapping away on his phone ordering pizza, and Mum is talking about me and jewellery and how I don't want to wear it any more, and Rich is trusting us to put all the pieces away because that's what you do when you love people – you trust them, and they trust you – I sweep the gold necklace, quickly, so quick nobody notices, into my hand and drop it into my shoe, right down the side, so I can walk upstairs and put it somewhere safe later. I can feel the point of the heart poking into my foot.

"All done!" I say when everything else is in place.

"Are we?" says Mum. I can see her checking over the slots, but I distract her quickly by saying, "Can we get your jewellery out, Mum?" And she looks so surprised that she forgets to check all the slots, gets up to fetch her jewellery box, and I close the lid of the case just as Rich puts his phone down and says, "Pizza's on its way."

"You have to try on Mum's jewellery too," I say, smiling as I see him lock up his case. He didn't even think to check it. It was as easy as that. And I did it by pretending to do nice things with Mum and Rich.

I'm a real thief now.

CHAPTER 11

When I get to Marie's house before school my heart feels like it will explode from my chest.

Marie's dad answers the door. He's in a uniform. He's a security officer in the shopping centre. I wonder if he's got any clue about what Marie gets up to.

"Ah, you must be Willow," he says, and smiles. "Marie's mentioned you recently. Glad she's made a new friend. Good to get her away from that Tay Welding. Dan's already here."

So Marie's dad doesn't know they're still friends. I say nothing. Although I don't like hearing someone say something bad about Tay. And I'm a bit disappointed that Dan is here. I was looking forward to walking to school with just Marie. I should have known.

In Marie's bedroom, which is decorated in lilac and cream with posters of singers and film stars from now, not from the past, all over it, Marie is doing her hair, and Dan is eating a packet of spicy Nik Naks.

"Want some?" he says to me as I walk in. His pockets are full of stolen snacks, as always.

"Morning, Willow!" says Marie, working on the plait that sweeps across her face. "Did you get it?"

No "How are you?" No "How are you feeling?" No anything. Just "Did you get it?"

"I got it," I say, and reach into my pocket where the necklace is burning a hole in my skin, right next to Nanna's photo. It almost feels like she's spying on me and I wonder why I haven't taken it out. "Here."

Marie's eyes go wide, like she's seen something magical.

"Corrr!" she says. She reaches out and grabs it. Isn't careful. And before I know it, she's wrapped it around her wrist and is holding it up to the light.

"Are those stones ... real?" she says. She must not know as much about these things as she says she does if she can't tell these stones are glass. I realise I don't even know if the jewellery itself is made of gold, or something like it, something pretend.

"No," I snap. "Of course not." She looks surprised at my reaction. "But that necklace is worth a hundred pounds."

"That's amazing, well done," says Marie. "We can give it to Tay later."

"I thought you said Dan would sell it," I say.

"She'll sell it," Marie corrects me. "She knows more of those sort of people than us." She's holding her wrist up and twisting it around, watching the heart and fake gems as they shiver.

"And give the money to Age UK?" I say.

"Oh, what is it with you and Age UK?" she says, almost laughing. "You obsessed with old people, or what?"

Dan sniggers.

I stand with my mouth open.

"I am not obsessed with old people," I say calmly. "I just thought—"

"Yes, yes, she'll give the money to Age Obsessed," she says. "Whatever. Well done. Next stage unlocked. We can talk about our next dare on the way to school."

"Sure you don't want some Nik Naks?" says Dan.

"I'm sure," I say.

As we leave Marie's house, her dad says, "Don't forget you're going to the childminder after school. She'll pick you up. I'm working a late shift."

Marie rolls her eyes and looks at me. "I'm eleven years old. Doesn't he know I'm too old for a childminder?" But over her shoulder she calls out, "Yes, Dad, of course! Have a good day."

He blows her a kiss and then we're out on the pavement.

At the beginning of *Singin' in the Rain*, Gene Kelly's character, Don Lockwood, is asked by a reporter to tell the story of how he became such a big star. The way he talks about it makes it sound amazing and glamorous, but the audience sees a series of scenes of him clowning around and getting into acting almost by mistake. He says that "Dignity, always dignity" is his motto, but all the scenes in that opening bit show the opposite of whatever dignity is. It turns out he got his first big role opposite Lina Lamont – who was already a big star – because he was able to take a punch and do a good stunt roll over a bar.

It's clever really. And funny. Someone who is looked up to by everyone, who is secretly someone very different underneath.

I watch Marie as we walk. I watch Dan. Marie is still wearing the necklace. I wonder when she's going to give it to Tay, and why she's not got me to give it to her this time. Maybe she's going to pretend she stole the necklace herself? *She'd better not.* I haven't gone through all this for someone else to take the credit.

As we walk into school together, I notice the way people look at Marie and Dan. I thought they looked up to them. But maybe it's not that. Maybe it's fear.

It's too late though, because as we walk through the main entrance I see Tay. Tay with the quiff and the confidence, who calls me Cricket Bat, and who's running this whole thing. It will all be worth it when she realises I've got it in me to steal big things. I have to stop myself running up to her and saying, "Look! Look at Marie's wrist! I took that! I did it!"

But I don't. Because it's a secret. And because Marie has taken the necklace off and is walking towards Tay. She can't be going to give it to her right there, in front of everyone as they're bundling into school?

She walks right up to Tay, stands there behind her and I see her reach out and open the side pocket of Tay's bag and drop something in. She turns to me and waggles her eyebrows and does a "shhhh" motion with her finger, showing me her bare wrist. Tay turns round, just as Marie has finished sealing the pocket back up.

"What do you want?" she says, looking at Marie, who smiles innocently.

"Nothing at all, thank you very much," says Marie. Dan sniggers.

"Get out of my way, will you? It's bad enough I see you at that stupid club all the time. I don't want to see you at school."

"That's not very kind, is it?" says Marie.

None of this adds up. Why is Tay acting like this? Why are Marie and Dan laughing? If this is their way of hiding what they're really up to at After School Crime Club, it's very convincing. It's like they actually hate each other.

"So," says Marie. "The next dare is a group project. You, me and Dan are going to take the sponsor money for The Big Walk from Mrs Emery's desk next week. We're going to distract her. And you're going to take it. You in?"

How is stealing money that's been brought in by school kids for a charity walk like being Robin Hood? How is this even anything like what they said it was? I think of Dan's pocketfuls of stolen snacks. I think of Marie saying I'm obsessed with old people. None of this sits right with me.

"I'm in," I say, despite my thoughts. Because I don't know what else to say.

The day goes by in a blur. I can't settle into my own skin. I can't feel right. Something is terribly wrong. And it's not just that I've stolen something from Rich, something I really shouldn't have. And it's not because I'm anything like Robin Hood.

Just before the end of the day I see Tay walking with Miss Wilde outside the window. Miss Wilde is looking very serious. Tay is looking at the ground, not walking with her usual swagger, her usual confidence. I look across the classroom at Marie and Dan and they are giggling.

What's going on?

What have I misunderstood?

Do you ever get the feeling that you've done something even more awful than you thought? A movie isn't always the poster. The hero is sometimes the villain. The villain is sometimes the hero.

And … which one am I?

CHAPTER 12

On Friday I walk by myself to After School (I can't say the word Crime now I'm actually committing them) Club. I don't want to talk to Marie, or Dan, or Brynn. I don't want to be around anybody. It starts to drizzle, but that doesn't make me feel like singing the "happy again" song. It just makes me feel wet and a bit cold. I'm amazed I actually get to The Book Box and don't just walk right past and go all the way home.

The others are already here. Well, everyone other than Tay, who is always last. The rest of the Club are muddled up, not in their usual groups.

Jed smiles, his usual over-the-top smile. He's wearing a jumper that has a Minecraft figure on it, I don't know which because I've never got into Minecraft. Rox isn't there yet, but I can smell her perfume, and see her fake fur jacket hung up on the hat stand next to the counter. The mood is different somehow. Not bad, not angry, but it feels more like Jed and Rox are in charge, and the kids are not. *What if they're going to call me out about the stolen book?* I think, my skin pricking with heat. *What if I've been caught on CCTV, or someone's told on me, or Tay was so unimpressed she decided to make it sound like it was all my idea, or something worse?*

"Hey, guys," says Jed cheerfully, giving nothing away. "Mixing things up a bit today. Think we've all been getting used to working with the same people, so thought we'd take you out of your comfort zones a bit."

"It's out of my comfort zone being here," says Pav. But he laughs.

"And me," says Nish, who's already drawing little hearts on her sheet in purple gel pen.

"It's out of all of your comfort zones, I understand that," says Jed. "But we wouldn't be doing our jobs if we didn't keep pushing you to see things differently."

Nobody says anything to that.

I take the seat with Brynn on one side and Nish on the other. Nish smiles and says, "Do you want to borrow a gel pen? Makes it a bit more beautiful." And this makes me smile, so I say, "Yes, please."

When I look up, I see Marie is sitting next to Dan and a blank seat. Marie is scowling at me, a furious look on her face. She looks at Nish and then back at me. Is … she … jealous? Whatever it is, I don't like it.

I feel suddenly glad that Jed and Rox have changed the tables. On the walk here I didn't feel as excited as I thought I would do. I felt flat. And a bit sick. And like there is a big mystery I need to solve, but I don't have all the pieces or even know where to start. But I do know that Marie is starting to get on my nerves, with all her rules and tests and telling me what to do. I thought the whole point of this club was to not let adults tell you what to do. But now I've got Marie, and Dan – and Tay without even saying anything telling me what to do. And it feels worse.

"Rox is just getting some snacks and hot chocolate," says Jed. "So while we wait for her, please read through the text in front of you and circle or highlight anything that stands out, anything that seems important, or anything that you don't understand."

Ha, I think, picking up the green gel pen Nish has passed me. *That'll be everything.*

And then I read the passage. It's from one of Charles Dickens' books about a boy called Oliver Twist who lived in Victorian times and is really poor and ends up joining a gang of other kids in order to survive. In the passage, it looks like he's in big trouble. It looks like the other kids are asking him to steal something.

"This is all so dramatic," says Nish with a shrug, circling the words *Angels that rest in heaven* with her gel pen. "Going on about angels in heaven. Poor kid." She double-underlines the word *rest*. "He just needs a rest, don't you think? He's never had much. Not the kind of rest you get with a clean duvet and your favourite things around you and your mum cooking goulash downstairs and the smell of the bath bubbles."

"No. He hasn't," I say. I feel the words in the text like a gunshot. *Steal.*

I look up at Jed, and he is looking at me. Does he know? Is he waiting for me to confess? I almost feel the words come out of my mouth. But if I say I did it, I will get Marie into trouble, and Dan. And, even worse, Tay. Everyone knows Tay is trouble. She'll get into more trouble than the rest of us.

Brynn turns to me from the other side and says, out of nowhere, "You shouldn't hang out with Marie and Dan. They're not what you want to get into."

"Pardon?"

"I've been wanting to talk to you for ages."

"You have?" The gel pen is shaking between my fingers, like it's made of actual jelly.

"Yeah," says Brynn. "They're not the sort of friends you want. Dan used to be all right, but he's changed. Everyone changes when they start hanging with her."

I don't say anything. I wonder when "her" will turn up, and if she's really worth all this angst. How does Tay get people to do things? Why do I want to do things that I would never usually do? I should have listened to my gut instinct.

I stare at the words on the page, all of them seeming to be about me, but also making me feel terrible that I have a roof over my head, and nice food, and loads of opportunities before me.

"I'll bear that in mind," I say. My head is full of everything, I'm not sure what I think or want to say. I'm still worried that Jed is about to expose me as the crook I am. And I still don't know what Tay's going to do with the stolen necklace. I'm still thinking about Marie's suggestion that we steal the sponsor money from Mrs Emery's desk, and the look on Tay's face when I asked her to sit with us at lunch the other day.

"Well, you should," says Brynn. "Because

there's nothing but trouble there, and I say that from experience." He turns to his sheet of paper and starts circling what look like random words.

Rox comes in with a tray of hot chocolate and a plate of brain-food biscuits. "So, any thoughts?" she asks the room. "What do we think of this extract?"

"There's a lot of God stuff," says Nish. "Lots of talking about angels and heaven. Like Oliver will have a terrible punishment if he steals. Like he's worried about his soul."

I look at her, and she smiles proudly. She whispers, "They love it when you point out God stuff."

She's right. They do. They're both lit up like their shop sign.

"Excellent!"

People start muttering but nobody offers any ideas. There's a tension in the air that you can almost taste. The hot chocolate doesn't take it away, although I take a big sip of mine, just in case.

The After School Crime Club. It suddenly seems such a babyish title I almost laugh. It's like they're trying to have their own little Victorian gang. And all it's about is stealing sweets, and books and jewellery. For no real reason.

Rox tells us to go work in pairs to discuss the extract and the rest of the session goes quietly, the rain whispering against the large glass windows at the front of the shop. I talk to Nish, who tells me about her cats and her little brother, and the roller disco she's going to next weekend.

"I'd love to learn how to roller skate," I say.

"Oh! You should come!" she says, easily as that. "I have my own skates, but you can rent them."

"Really?"

"Yeah! Ask your mum, or dad … or whoever you live with."

"I live with my mum," I say. "And with her boyfriend soon, when he changes jobs. I like him. My dad left when I was little. I don't really hear from him." That's more than I've said about my dad to anyone in a long time. Or maybe ever. Certainly more than I've ever said to Marie. "My nanna said I look like him."

Nish is looking at me kindly.

"It's the moustache!" I say, cracking a joke, because that's what always works with Mum.

"Ha!" says Nish. "It's good to laugh about stuff. But that's hard. That's a lot."

"It is," I say. "It's always been OK. I didn't really know him. I've always been close to my mum's mum, my nanna. But…" I stop there. I can't tell her the rest, or I will cry.

While we are talking, I realise Marie has wandered over on the pretence that she's getting some stationery from the shared pots. She never uses stationery from the shared pots. She always has tons of her own. As she does it, she leans against our table. I see her, right there, as she picks up Nish's packet of gel pens and slips them into the big pocket of her school hoodie. The look she gives me says, "It's as easy as that, Willow."

But I feel angry.

She steals from other kids? Kids who might have saved up for things, or been given things by other people? And she'll want me to do the same?

Nish is still smiling, and she's being kind to me. Listening. Asking me about things. What has she done to deserve being stolen from? She likes the pens because they make things look more beautiful. She told me so. How can we be the good guys in this situation if we're taking things from someone like her?

And then next week Marie wants me to help her steal the sponsor money? The money that people have given kids for going on a fundraising walk, and which will be used to do some good?

Marie looks pretty happy though, and Dan is looking at her adoringly.

It's then that Tay arrives, really late. She comes in, without her bag this time, and stands in the doorway.

"Sorry I'm late," she says. "I had to visit someone. It was important." She hasn't got her usual swagger, and she's wet from the rain. I was feeling angry with her a minute ago, for getting me involved in this stupid After School Crime Club, but she just looks pitiful now, and I feel sorry for her. Everything she gets is because people are afraid of her. Or want to impress her. When does she ever get to be herself?

"I hope all's OK, Tay. There's a seat next to Marie," says Jed. "Marie, will you pop back to your seat, so you can get Tay up to speed."

Marie walks back to her seat, as though Nish's

pens aren't glowing through the fabric of her hoodie.

"When hell freezes over," says Tay, "will I work with Marie."

"Tay!" says Rox – angrily, for her. "What an awful thing to say."

"Awful people deserve to be told awful things," says Tay. "I'd rather work alone than with her. Else I'm out of here."

Jed and Rox share a look like they don't know what to do.

"Um…. Nish, would you mind sitting next to Tay, and, Marie, you take Nish's spot, if that's OK with everyone."

Nish gets up, seemingly unaware her pens are missing, and – confusingly – quite happy to go and work with Tay. "I liked working with you," she says. "Think about the skating and tell me next time. It would be fun!"

Why is she being nicer to me than my supposed friends and now fellow club members? Things feel all back to front.

"It's all an act," hisses Marie, and she drops down into Nish's seat as though she hasn't just taken her pens. "Tay only pretends she hates me so people don't know what we're up to."

"It's very convincing," I say. I can hear Brynn's words in my head. Something isn't right here.

"Oh, Tay is very good at what she does," says Marie admiringly. "I'd have thought you'd have noticed that by now."

Nish and Tay are suddenly having a heated conversation and it's definitely not about the text. "But she seems nice!" says Nish. "I like her!"

"Well, I don't. So if she's coming skating, then I'm not."

"But…!" Nish looks over at me, guiltily. They're talking about me? Why are they talking about me? And why is Tay going skating with Nish? Nish isn't part of the After School Crime Club. And why is Tay being so horrible when all I've ever done since coming to this place is what she asked?

Brynn says, "Are you starting to get it now…?" And I look at him, very confused.

"She's a sheep," says Tay suddenly, her words hitting me like an arrow. "She'll do anything to fit in. Doesn't really care about people."

How can she be talking about *me*?

Is this the next challenge? To prove I'm not a sheep? Because I'm over proving things to Marie, or to Dan, and even to Tay. I'm through proving anything. If nobody in this so-called After School Crime Club is actually going to be nice to me for more than five minutes, if they're never going to say "well done", if they're not even going to hang around with me, what is the point of being part of it? Nish is the one person who's actually shown an interest in me and my life without asking for anything, and now Tay's trying to turn her against me.

I was happier before all this ever started.

So I stand up and walk right over to Tay and Nish. I'll let Nish see what sort of people they all are. What sort of person I am. I'm out. I'm sick of the little tests and codes, and I'm done with them.

"Nish, Marie took your gel pens. She did it for Tay." I look Tay right in her brown-spark eyes. "I'm not going to be part of this any longer. I hope you're happy now."

And she stares at me, open mouthed, while Marie is shaking her head furiously, and maybe even looking a bit *scared*, in the background, and the colour has drained from Dan's face. And Nish just looks confused. I'm done with this club. I'm done with all of them.

Then I turn around and stare at Marie. Right in the eyes. And I don't smile, or frown, or do anything. I just stare right at her as I swing my bag on to my shoulder like I've not got a care in the world, as though I've always stood up for myself. I'm through with her lecturing me, and telling me what I have to prove. I choose my own rules, and my own behaviour, and she can like it or not. I don't even care.

And that's when I see Tay, still in her seat staring at me with her mouth open like she's seeing me for the first time. I don't care. I don't care if Tay Welding never speaks to me again.

And I look her straight in the eye. I do not turn away as I push past her, and everyone else, and leave the shop all by myself, thank you very much. I don't even say thank you and goodbye to Rox and Jed. And I feel powerful.

CHAPTER 13

That night, I sleep like a baby. A deep sleep that feels like I'm on a boat on a gentle ocean. No dreams. No waking up. Nothing other than blissful, uninterrupted rest.

The next morning, I feel like a new person.

As I put on my clothes, I decide that I will go to Nanna's. I never usually go and see her in the morning by myself, only with Mum when we're sorting her stuff. Sorting her stuff for Age UK. When we're doing that I hate not having the time to imagine Nanna there. I hate being rushed and I hate rushed goodbyes more than I hate most things. I always think, what if that's the last time I see that person, and the last thing I did was rush off to do something else?

Never rush a goodbye, says Nanna's voice in my head.

Then I think. *You always rush your goodbyes with Mum.*

Mum is in the kitchen washing up. She's looking out at the back garden, humming to the radio. She's wearing a really nice pair of trousers, pinstriped, and a lilac fluffy jumper. She's curled her hair, and it sits on her shoulders, flicked out in all directions, and it seems shinier than usual.

She's wearing the slippers Rich bought her on his visit to Iceland a few years ago.

"Mum," I say, walking up beside her. "How are you?"

It sounds funny, me just saying it like that, just walking up to her in the kitchen and asking how she is. It's not something I would usually ask. I usually take part in the pretence that everything is OK, everything has always been OK, even while Mum's swinging back and forth between absolute neat perfectionism and utter devastation. We both know that one of the reasons I've not had friends home, back when other children were visiting each other's houses with their parents, was that Mum didn't want anyone to see where we lived. And then they stopped asking. And then it felt like it was something to do with me.

"I think I'm OK," says Mum. "I think I am."

"You should say if you're not," I say. "We used to talk about things all the time. Do you remember when we'd go to the park after school, and you'd help me climb over the top of the climbing frame? The big arch? And I'd get stuck at the top, standing on the top of the arch, and you'd put your arms up, and you'd say, 'You can just fall through the gap and I'll catch you. I'll always catch you'. And I'd slip through the gap, and you would. You would always. And one day, you said it but I kept going, I kept climbing over the arch and all the way down the other side. And you clapped and cheered and said, 'Well done, Willow. I knew you could do it'."

Mum turns and looks at me. She's got tears in her eyes. "I remember that," she says quietly.

"You always made me think I could do anything I wanted, and if I didn't … it would be OK. But…" I stop. What is it I want to say to her? I think of old movies where the character learns to stand up for themselves, or says the thing they couldn't say before, or they fall in love with life and being themselves, and get to dance, dance, dance, right up to the end credits.

"I still think you can do anything you want," she says. "I think you could do anything."

"But it never feels enough," I say. "I feel like I'm always supposed to be more than I ever could be. And I just … can't."

Mum stares at me. She looks so pretty in the light from the window. I realise it's been so long since I talked to her about my feelings, it feels strange to be doing it now. But I can't help myself. Something about yesterday at After School Club has changed things. Like I got full to the brim with feelings and now they are all flowing out of me and don't know how to stop.

"You are always enough," says Mum. And we look at each other, standing on the cold lino, neither of us knowing what to say next. I sort of feel it's her turn. But she doesn't say anything else, and instead she turns round and carries on with the washing up. She's put in too much washing-up liquid and the bubbles look like something from a cartoon when a room is going to be flooded with bubbles. Mum doesn't seem to notice. The moment has passed, and I think, maybe she'll never really notice anything important about me again. And this makes me feel so sad, like all the best things about us are in the past, and there's nothing I can do.

"I'm going to see Nanna," I say. "In the *cemetery*. Do you want to come with me?"

Mum doesn't turn round. "Not today, love," she says. I can't see her expression because her face is towards the window and I nearly give up hope of us saying the things we need to say, and doing the things we need to do, to make things good between us. But she adds, "But I will soon. We'll go together. We'll buy flowers, and cake, and we'll sit with her together. And talk about all the times we've had. We will. I know I have to. And I will. I promise. But not today."

She turns round then, and I almost think she's going to hug me. But she reaches out and tucks my hair behind my ear and says, "Look at you. Beautiful girl." She has not called me beautiful girl in a long time. The words surprise me, like she's speaking a different language. And I say, "I hope it's soon, Mum. I need you to come."

I hope she'd feel the same about if me if she found out what I've done.

And then, without us saying any more, I make a flask of tea and put it into my backpack. I've still got some chocolate in there from the other day, but I put some more in, from the cupboard next to the sink, right next to Mum. She doesn't say anything else, and neither do I. Then I turn around and leave the kitchen.

And the house.

Mum has always wanted me to be good at something. To become exceptional at something.

Well, I found something I could be good at. It was so easy to take the toy, the book, the necklace. But it's illegal, it's wrong. Everyone knows stealing is wrong. It's in the ten commandments. And I know I don't believe in God, but ... everyone knows it's wrong. Everyone. Including me. Especially stealing from people who've been kind to you.

I can't be part of the After School Crime Club. That much I know. At the moment, I don't know much else.

I'm glad there's no Club today. I've never been so glad to go and see Nanna in my life, and as I walk, so many thoughts are swirling in my head. Marie telling me to steal something from the shop for Tay. Marie telling me to steal the necklace, for Tay, for charity. Me doing it. Actually doing it.

And the dare I could never have done. Steal the money that kids had brought in for charity? Right from under Mrs Emery's nose?

And Tay. The look on her face. The disgust. The confusion. The pain?

There must be another way to make friends. To choose the right friends. I think of Nish. It was so easy to talk to her. And she asked about me. Has Marie ever asked me anything about my life, or the things I like? I'm pretty sure she hasn't.

I walk past Nanna's house, and round the corner to the gate of the cemetery. Some people would hate living there. Nanna loved it. "I am OK with life coming to an end," she said to me. "I like to think of all the people who came before. And I like to think of all the people who'll come after." It's such a big thought. All the people who've ever lived. All the people who ever will live. Like a giant chorus line.

If there is a heaven, and I'm not sure yet if there is, it would be like a musical. And there'd be singing, no matter the weather. There would always be singing in the rain.

It's not hard to find Nanna's grave. It's a nice black headstone. Shiny. And there are flowers, pink carnations, Nanna's favourite, in a special vase with holes. Fresh ones. I can't think who's put them there if Mum hasn't been coming.

Rich, I think. It has to be. I feel a flash of guilt. About stealing the necklace. About what else I might have gone on to do if I hadn't snapped yesterday.

I get out the chocolate and the flask of tea. I pour out a mug for me and a cup for Nanna. I don't imagine her saying anything this time. I don't even pretend she's put the kettle on or try to visualise what it was like in her kitchen, the sound of her slippers on the lino, of her hair, which she never had cut short like her other friends, but kept long, plaited and then turned up into a twist. Like Grace Kelly. "Got to keep some things the same," she'd say. "I'm never having my hair cut like an old lady. Why do we do it? To become more acceptable? I don't want to be acceptable, Willow. I want to be me." I thought she was beautiful. Her eyes. Her smile. The fact I knew I could trust her, that she'd never trick me, or be cruel, or pretend, or lie. Or steal.

Shame spreads throughout me like I've had a bucket of hot water thrown over me. I can't even eat a square of chocolate.

The birds are loud today, their little songs, and loud chirps. The trees let light through them, and the cemetery is full of new life. Flowers, the scuttle of little creatures in the undergrowth. I've spent more time at Nanna's house than anywhere else over the past three months. I've spent more time there than at home. I've been worried that if I don't come, everything will slip away. The memories. The sound of Nanna's voice. The smells from her kitchen. The way she set out her perfume and her silver-plated hairbrush and her make-up on the special mat she'd sewn when she was young.

Each time I go to her house, the smell gets more faint. She gets more faint. And soon someone else will live there entirely.

I'm worried it will take too much effort to remember. And I'm so afraid of forgetting.

Nanna's grave is neat, but I pick a few weeds that have popped up anyway. It doesn't seem real that she's not in the world as she was. Her body and brain and her words, all gone. I don't want it to be true, but here is the grave, which is clean and simple and says *Elsie Eleanor Fry, Mother, Nanna, much loved and missed* and has a quote from *High Society*, Nanna's favourite film: *There are fairies at the bottom of my garden all ringing little bells.* Grace Kelly's character Tracy Lord says it. When I read it there, it makes me think of all the things Nanna said and loved, and it makes me want to look for fairies at the bottom of the garden too. To look for magic.

"Nanna," I say. "I know you can hear me. I hope

you can." The leaves rustle in the background, like she's telling me she can. I like all those stories about people becoming elements when they die. Air. Water. Fire. Earth. They make sense to me. "I've been doing some things I'm not proud of, and I don't know why. I would have talked to you about it properly. I kept thinking … that … you'd come and tell me what to do, somehow. That you'd step in and say, 'Willow, this isn't the way to go about things,' but you never did. But I knew that was what you'd say. And now I'm in a muddle. I don't know what to do. And I'm sorry I stole the otter and the book and the necklace. I thought it would make things better, but it made everything worse."

The tea tastes thin and watery. Not my best work. Nanna's cup sits there, full.

"I just wanted something to happen. Something different. I wanted to know how to live now you're not here. But I got it wrong." I feel good saying that. I did get it wrong. It's not too late to fix it. I can get the book back from Tay, because I'm pretty sure it didn't go to Age UK, and I can put it back on the shelf. I can get the necklace back too and give it to Rich. And if I'm feeling really brave,

I can talk to Jed and Rox about what happened. And I could ask one of them to help me. I think I trust Rox, at least. I think she'd understand. Maybe.

"Mum says she's going to come and see you soon. I really hope she does. I think she misses you. She's not been the same since you died. It's like she's switched something off. And I miss her too."

This makes me well up. I never cry. It's not because I think crying's bad, it's just that I worry that if I start crying, I might never stop, and then what would I do? I quickly rub my eyes.

It's then that I'm aware of a presence in the graveyard. Not a spectre or something. Not Nanna. But a real person, moving along the hedge at the far end, where the slightly older graves are. And I jolt, wipe my eyes, and look.

This time I know it is Tay.

She is carrying her big bag, and she's got her headphones on. I watch her this time, don't hide, don't curl up into a ball. And then she looks up and sees me, sat beside Nanna's grave with my badly prepared tea party, and does a double take. She has flowers in her hands. A big bunch of chrysanthemums: pink, yellow, red. She's combed her hair into a perfect quiff. She looks smart, and she is looking at me. I don't look away.

Tay Welding visits somebody in the graveyard too. Her bag is full of flowers and picnic food. She looks away from me and starts to set it out. This seems more surprising to me than anything else that's been happening these past weeks. All the times I've imagined what Tay carries in her bag: stolen goods, weapons, dead bodies.

I think, *Should I go over and say something? But what would I say?*

But Tay stays looking away and sits down, right over there beside someone's grave, with her back to me.

The breeze is soft on my skin as I tidy up the tea things. *Everything is different now*, I think. *I'm different now. Nanna isn't going to help you work out what to do. You'll have to do it yourself.*

"What I've done is not that bad. Is it, Nanna? Taking a cuddly toy, a book, a necklace. Not compared to murder or hurting someone, or just being mean?"

Nanna doesn't reply. Of course. And I don't imagine a reply either. I let my words hang in the air, heard only by the birds and the plants and the trees.

The sound of her saying nothing sounds like she's loudly saying, "You know it's that bad, Willow, and you're not getting anything from me to tell you otherwise. You know what's right and wrong. You don't need me to tell you."

But she doesn't understand. Nobody understands. I do need her to tell me. I need her to tell me what to do. I need her to spell it out and give me a cuddle, and I need to walk away from her sure of what's going to happen next.

But she still says nothing. She will never say anything again. And then I do cry. I cry for what feels like a long time. How do human beings cope with all the things they lose? How does Mum? Dad walked away and never came back. And now she's lost her mum. And she still curls her hair and puts on perfume and makes pasta dinners for me and Rich. And my dad emails me sometimes, but never much. And he never asks about Mum. Like she's disappeared from his story altogether.

I stand up to leave, and that's when Tay stands up too. She doesn't put away her picnic. She doesn't touch her stuff. But she walks over to me and Nanna. She walks right towards me, and I think, I don't want to be called a sheep in front of Nanna. I don't want her to see Tay be awful to me. How could I have ever wanted to be friends with someone who makes other people do things they don't want to do?

I puff myself up and take two steps away from Nanna. I set my jaw like I've seen people do in movies when they are about to have a fight. Will me and Tay fight, properly fight, among the graves? The thought makes my fast heartbeat return.

"Willow," says Tay.

"I saw you," I say. "That day. When I was over there." I gesture to Nanna's garden. I don't say that I thought maybe she'd followed me. Or that I thought she had a bag full of stolen goods. We stand there looking at each other. I can't believe I let her tell me what to do these past weeks. I can't believe she used Marie to get me to do what she couldn't tell me to do herself.

"I'm sorry I called you a sheep," she says. "Marie can be persuasive."

"I just wanted to…"

"What? What have you and Marie and Dan

been up to? She's a nasty piece of work. She's told people so much stuff about me. None of it's true."

And I feel the words fall out of my mouth. I don't even stop when I see Tay's face change to pure rage.

"I came to After School Club, and I just ... really liked you. I wanted to be your friend. I've never wanted to have a friend before. And then Marie started being nice to me. And she said that you wanted me to be part of your gang, and if I wanted to be part of it, I had to pass some tests. The first test was to steal something that wouldn't be missed. The second was to steal something from The Book Box and then give it to you. She said you'd give it to a charity shop. I chose the cricket book because you said you liked cricket. She said if I passed enough tests, did enough dares, then I'd prove I was good enough to be friends with you and her and Dan and Brynn, and the next test was stealing some jewellery from my mum's boyfriend, Rich – he goes around getting shops to stock posh jewellery. And I did it. I did. And Marie had said we'd sell it and give the money to Age UK, but she changed her mind.

And I thought you'd be happy with me. But you called me a sheep. So I just … stopped trying to fit in. So I told Nish that Marie had stolen her pens for you. I want you to stop telling me what to do. I'm not stealing any more stuff. And I'm not taking the sponsor money from Mrs Emery's desk. Because I can't. No matter how much I want you to like me."

I do not get the response I am expecting. I am expecting her to call me a chicken or a coward or a failure. To tell me I'd never be good enough for her gang anyway. But she doesn't. I've never seen anyone look so confused and so much like they suddenly understand a ton of things they really couldn't understand before. I think, *Is she going to hit me?* and I recoil a bit. She looks hurt when I do.

"You are just like everybody else," she says. "You stole a book because Marie told you I wanted you to. You didn't stop to think if Marie was telling the truth. You didn't stop to think maybe the stories you heard about me weren't true. You just did it. You say you wanted to be my friend, but you didn't want to be my friend. You wanted to impress Tay Welding, the story.

Like everyone does. You didn't even try to get to know me first. Or find out what I want. Or who I am."

I am stung. She's right. I didn't. All this time I wanted to impress her, I never once stopped to think, does she even want me to impress her? I believed Marie because it never crossed my mind not to. Because I believed all the things I'd heard about Tay Welding, and never once tried to see if they were true. I feel ashamed. And sorry. And like, I knew there was more to Tay, but I was too much of a coward to find any of it out.

"I'm sorry," I say. It sounds small and pathetic and nowhere near enough.

"I've never stolen anything in my life," says Tay. "Not one thing."

"Well, that's good to know," I say, with a little laugh. But I feel awful.

Tay smiles, slightly, then sets her face back to anger. "You should have talked to me, Willow. I thought you might be different. Nish said she thinks you're different. She's the only one who's ever talked to me like I'm not a bad guy in a story. She's a real friend."

I think of Nish and her circles over her i's and j's.

were, I wasn't being honest with myself.

Tay looks at Nanna's grave. "Is that your nan?"

I nod. Then I feel brave. I've nothing else to lose. "Who do you visit here?"

"My mum," says Tay. "My mum died when I was in Year Two. And then I went to live with my big sister."

There is a moment of silence. Then I say, "I should have talked to you properly."

Tay considers this. "Well..." she says. "My counsellor says I put up a lot of walls. So I guess I don't make it easy."

"That's very kind of you to say," I say. "But I was an idiot."

Tay laughs but she doesn't disagree.

"You know," she says. "I came over here to be angry with you. But I don't feel angry any more."

That's a relief. *See, Nanna? She's not angry with me.* After everything, Tay's opinion of me still matters. In fact, it matters more.

"But we need to think what we can do about Marie," says Tay. "She is totally the villain in all of this. I could stand here and argue with you all day, but she used the way you were feeling about all this –" She waves her arm towards Nanna's grave – "to trick you. She played with your feelings."

I nod. It's true. The very thought of it makes me feel sick.

"Why did you want to impress me so much anyway?" says Tay.

I don't know what to say to that. Anything I do say will be embarrassing. I liked you. I wanted, more than anything, to just be near you, and never stopped to think why.

"There's just something about you, I guess," I say. "Not the stuff about flushing people's heads down toilets. Just something about the way you always seem to be yourself. I want to always be myself. I admire you."

I feel the redness spread over me. It's so embarrassing to be saying this, but not saying this will be worse. Hiding how I feel has got me nowhere.

"Well. I kind of feel the same about you," says Tay. "You and your burger sweatshirt, and the way you sit in the playground by yourself, and it never seemed to bother you. And the way you were sitting in your nanna's garden, like she still matters, like you're never going to let her not matter."

"She will always matter."

"I'd like you to come skating with me and Nish," says Tay.

"I'd like that."

Then Tay goes over to her bag, gets out the book about cricket, comes back over to Nanna's grave and says, "I think it's best you have this back." I take it like it's made of fire. It burns. And then I remember the necklace.

"I saw you talking to Miss Wilde yesterday. You weren't in trouble, were you?" I panic.

"No, I wasn't. We were just talking. She kind of gets me now. I guess that's what talking does…"

"Phew!" I say. "I thought maybe Marie had said you'd taken the necklace. Look in your side pocket! The little one."

"What?"

"Look!" Tay unzips the pocket I saw Marie slip the necklace into yesterday, and pushes in her hand. Out comes the chain, with the gold heart and sparkly gems glinting in the light by Nanna's grave. She holds it there, and we both look at it.

She drops it into my open palm.

"I wasn't trying to frame you," I say quickly. "Marie put it there. She said you'd told her to."

"I can guess," says Tay. "Marie is… Well. Always Marie. I didn't know anything about it, but I think you know that." She smiles as I hold the necklace tight, thinking, maybe I really can fix this. "I'm going to finish having breakfast with my mum if that's OK. I'll introduce you to her, one time. Maybe. If you'd like."

"I would like. And I'll introduce you to Nanna."

"That's a deal," she says. Then Tay Welding, someone I've longed to be friends for so long but actually knew nothing about, turns back to her picnic, and I step away, step over the moss and the grass and the sun patches. And I walk away from Nanna, suddenly more sure of what's going to happen next.

CHAPTER 14

It takes a lot for me to go into school on Monday but I do. I'm not sure how. But I do.

My usual seat next to Marie is occupied by another girl called Jenny, and I look to see my old spot empty, near the window, next to nobody. I sat there for so long, and never once thought about the fact I didn't have a work partner. Jack and Evan, who sit at the table in front, would turn around and we'd be a three if there was group work.

Funny to look back at something that meant so little at the time and feel a pang of missing how it was.

I sit in my old seat and look out of the window. I can see three seagulls on the playground scaring all the other birds away. I name them Jerry, Henri and Lise, after the characters in *An American in Paris*. I watch them perform their song-and-dance numbers. The school playground is 1950s Paris and Henri, the seagull, is trying to make it as a musician, while Jerry sells his art. Lise is wonderful and complicated. In this scene, she is ignoring Jerry and picking at somebody's dropped orange peel. She is hungry.

Marie hasn't said anything to me this morning,

it's like I'm not even here.

I can't stop thinking about how she lied about Tay.

I've learned so much this last couple of weeks, without even thinking I wanted to. I've also learned that when I like somebody, I will do anything for them, even if it isn't right for me. And I don't know what to do with that knowledge. It sort of scares me. I thought I knew me better.

I do my work quietly. I have some plans for After School Club. I know exactly what I'm going to do. I haven't spoken to Tay about it, but I don't need her approval. I just need my own.

At lunch the dinner hall is loud. There's lots of chatter and laughing and whooping when somebody drops their tray. I go to sit in my old space, as always, and I hope the Year 3s and 4s join me instead of Marie. But I see her and Dan walking towards me with their trays and I think, *I wish they'd just keep ignoring me*, but that's too easy, I know.

Marie sits opposite me, and Dan too. They take out their ketchup and it doesn't seem impressive any more. It's just a silly little action to show they don't care. But they do care. They care what people think of them more than the people who follow the rules do.

"So…" says Marie. She smiles brightly all of a sudden, and I'm thrown by how easily she can switch it on. Her hair bounces as she moves her head, ponytail swinging, her swept-over fringe falling across her eye.

"So…" I say. I smile. I don't feel awkward, or angry even. I know exactly what she is. I can *see* her, at last.

"You really messed up at Club on Friday. It's taken ages to fix it with Tay. And I had to show Nish I'd picked up her pens by mistake. She's way too much of a goody-goody to be part of our club."

She still thinks I think Tay has organised the whole thing. She doesn't know about the graveyard, and the roller skating, and how I know Tay Welding has never stolen a thing in her entire life. I feel powerful.

"I know…" I say. Wow, I can act. "I'm sorry. I lost my nerve. I didn't want to get into trouble."

"Exactly," says Marie. "All the things Tay thought about you before I convinced her to let you join the After School Crime Club. You did *exactly* what she said you would, and it was nearly impossible to convince her otherwise after that whole shambles. And I had to explain everything to Rox and Jed after you left The Book Box. Tay stormed off soon after you. I had to say you two had fallen out and I said I'd picked up Nish's gel pens by mistake. They bought it, obviously. Because they're so caught up in being good people, they notice nothing. But now you have to prove to me it wasn't a waste of my time. You'll have to help us get the sponsorship money. I heard Mrs Emery say there is nearly two hundred pounds in there!" She looks excited.

"I'm sorry, Marie," I say. She was right about cheating. It is fun. Sometimes. When you're cheating someone who's already cheated you.

"Well… I forgive you, obviously. As does Dan. Don't you, Dan?"

Dan nods and shoves some ketchup-covered chips into his mouth.

"But… I don't think I can do that for you again. Another outburst like that and you're out. It's too much effort. You're either one of us or you're not."

"I'm one of you," I say immediately. "Just tell me what I need to do, and I'll do it." Wow. This version of Willow is what I nearly became. How can that happen?

"There's too much attention on us today after your little outburst so we'll do it tomorrow. At lunch. Dan and I will distract Mrs Emery, and you'll go to her desk and get the money. And then we'll talk about what comes next. You understand there will have to be more tests now? You can't just be part of the club after getting a few things right. You really messed up. I'm doing you a favour."

Why is it that when anyone tells you they are doing you a favour, they are actually trying to make you do *them* a favour? *When you do something nice for someone, you don't need to keep reminding them about it.* I don't even wonder if that's what Nanna would say. It's what I say. And what I say counts.

"I understand," I say. "And I'm sorry."

I really should be an actor. I must have got the pitiful, willing-to-please act exactly right because Marie says, "Oh you're so sweet, it's hard to be cross with you. But you've got to grow a thicker skin. Otherwise you'll get us all in trouble."

"I know," I say.

"Good," she says. "We walking to Club after school?"

I don't want to. I want to walk by myself. Or even get a lift with Mum. But for now I'll keep acting my role as Willow-Who-Does-What-Marie-Says. So I say, "Of course."

"Great!" says Marie. "Right. Gotta go." And she and Dan stand up, leaving their half-eaten food and their mess right there on the table. They don't care about anyone or anything. I can see it now. So I finish my food and clear up after all of us. I won't be sitting with them again.

When we get to The Book Box, the tables are still pushed into a big square. Everyone else is here, including Brynn, and including Tay, who's not late and is sitting next to Nish, who's using an ordinary biro. Neither of them look at me or say hello, and for a moment I feel nervous, like I can't do this by myself. But I know I can. I don't need back up. I just need me.

Mum sent me here to be a better version of myself, and it's worked. Just not in the way she thought.

"Hello, you three!" says Rox cheerfully. "Hot chocolate and muffins today. It's my birthday!"

Yikes. I don't want to make a scene on Rox's birthday but if I don't do something about it today, I'll never do something about it. Sorry, Rox.

"Happy birthday, Rox!" Marie and Dan and I say at the same time, and all three of us laugh. Somebody give me an Oscar and a Chanel gown, thank you very much.

"Thank you! Take a seat. We're going to do some maths."

"Multiplying fractions! Goody!" says Marie, looking at the papers on the desks, and she sits down, pulls out a gel pen and starts to work straight away. I look at the page and it's all blibs and blobs, of course. But. I'm sure there's a way to understand this. I look at the numerator and the denominator. At least I can remember which is which. I think.

I start to write some answers.

"That's wrong," says Marie, pointing at my workings-out. "And that."

"Oh," I say.

"Now, Marie," says Jed, appearing beside us in another of his brightly checked shirts. "There are kinder ways to say that."

"Urgh," says Marie. Her Nice Girl façade

slipping for a moment. "She just never gets it. No matter what I say."

"Maybe you've not found the way to say it that is right for Willow," says Jed. "Everyone's brain is different."

"Yeah. And some people's are better than others," she mutters under her breath. How could I have ever wanted to be friends with her, or listened to a single thing she said? And I know now's the time for me to do what I have to do. So I stand up, and cough a little, like I'm about to make a speech at a wedding, which is what this feels like. I have to get it right.

"I want to say something," I say, calmly, although my hands are shaking and my voice sounds like it's been speeded up on a computer.

"Of course!" says Rox kindly. "What is it?"

"I didn't want to come here," I say. A few people laugh.

"Oh, I know that," says Rox. "I understand."

"It's not that," I say. "I didn't want to come here because my mum was always saying I should be better at everything than I am. At least, that's what I thought she was saying." I look at Tay and Nish, and they are smiling at me. Tay nods. It's all the encouragement I need. "But I was happy as I was. I love old movies. Old musicals. Have you ever seen *Singin' in the Rain*? It's amazing. The dancing. The songs. The way the rain falls around the dancing. It's incredible."

"Great story, bro," laughs Dan. Marie giggles. But nobody else does. I look down at my bag.

"But there were some things I needed to change. Then I got caught up in something here that wasn't right for me. I got convinced I had to be a different person. And I'm not blaming anyone. I did that all by myself." I reach into my bag and pull out the book. It sits there, on the table in front of me, and Marie actually gasps. She tries to pull me down by my jumper sleeve, but I pull away.

"I was convinced to steal this book from here. I was told it would prove I was fearless and I could be part of something. And I wanted to be part of something. I've never felt part of something before."

Jed and Rox stand up. They are looking at each other, concerned. "I think we should talk about this in private," says Jed. "Because that's a big thing you've just said."

"I don't need to say it in private," I say, sure of myself. "I need to say it here." They let me continue. "But stealing the book didn't make me feel part of something. It made me feel alone. And it made me feel guilty. And it made me have to lie to people. So I'm giving it back, and I'll pay for it too, if it's not in perfect condition. And it's OK if you call the police, because I'll admit what I've done, and I'll take any punishment coming my way. Because anything is better than stealing from people who've been kind to you, and believing stuff people say about other people, without asking those people yourself how they are doing, and who they are."

I look at Tay. She looks at me. Nish has a big smile on her face. Tay starts to clap. And so does Nish. The two of them clap and the rest of us just watch them.

Nobody says anything for what feels like a long time, until eventually Rox says, "That was a brave thing you just did. I'm sad you stole the book. I'm glad you've brought it back. We don't need to call the police." She didn't have to even think. There was no pause. There was no maybe. Rox decided in that moment to think the best of me.

And I've never felt more grateful for anything in my life.

"If we can't learn from our mistakes, what can we learn from?" adds Jed.

Tay and Nish are smiling at me. The others are smiling. Then Pav, very quietly, says, "When I first came to After School Club, Marie told me I had to steal a book to prove to Nish that I was good enough to be in their gang."

"What?!" say Nish and Marie at the same time.

"And I did it," says Pav. "I've still got the book at home. It's about Ariana Grande."

"I *love* Ariana Grande," says Nish. Then, realising what's been said, "I would never have wanted you to steal something for me."

"I know," says Pav. "I realised not long after. I didn't know what to do."

"Marie told me to steal this book too," I say. "She said it would impress Tay." I feel myself go red as I say that, but *in for a penny, in for a pound*, Nanna would say. I'll have no secrets left by the end of this. And I'm still shaking.

"And the worst thing is I believed her because I thought I knew all about Tay Welding. But I didn't. And I regret it. And I'm sorry. For everything."

Marie stands up, throws her arms in the air, and Dan looks up at her. "This is absolute rubbish!" she says. "I'm not going to sit here and listen to this. It's a bunch of lies. And I'll make sure my dad comes in and gets an apology."

"Marie," says Jed carefully. "I will definitely be talking to your dad."

Marie's face clouds over for a moment then she's back to full-on defiant mode. "Good!" she says. "You'd better make sure you do. He will be having a full apology and maybe he'll sue you all for defamation of character. He knows all about how Tay used to steal things from Julie, our childminder."

"He can't do that if it's not true," says Brynn suddenly. "I've kept your secrets for ages. I remembered what you were like before, when you were nice, and we were friends. I kept thinking you'd go back to being like that again. But you never did. And when I saw you trying it on with Willow, when you knew she'd just lost her gran… I don't know you any more. I don't like who you've become. And what the others are saying is true."

Marie looks like she's been electric-shocked.

And so do I, probably. Brynn had been trying

to warn me. He wasn't jealous. He wasn't a happy member of the After School Crime Club. He was just a person whose friends took a wrong turn, and he was trying to work out what to do.

"I'm going now!" Marie says. And Dan gets up to go with her. "Not with *you*!" she says cruelly. "I don't want anything to do with any of you!" Dan looks genuinely hurt by that. But he gets up and follows after her anyway. Some habits are hard to break.

Jed and Rox don't try to stop them. They turn to us all and Rox says seriously, "I am so sorry this has been happening here, right under our noses. If any of you want to talk about this, at any time, you are most welcome. We will be talking to your parents and carers. We will make this OK. You should never be forced into doing things you don't want to do, for anyone. Ever."

It feels like the room lets out a big sigh. The books are whispering on the shelves. The fairy lights are twinkling. I have never felt so at ease in my entire life. Me. Willow Strong. Who never spoke up in class. Who'd avoid putting my hand up and hide in the corner. Who is average. Who likes plain cheese sandwiches, wearing my burger-wearing-sunglasses jumper on all occasions, who watches ripples on the lake. Who has tea parties by Nanna's grave. Who stole from Rich, but will make it all right. I did this.

"I'm sorry I said all that on your birthday," I say. "I just couldn't wait."

And Rox smiles at me then, bright, true. "Oh, it's never a bad day for the truth to come out. Some could say it's the best birthday present I've ever had." Her hair shines under the fairy lights. It's like she's magic. And I'm glad Mum made me come here. I might even tell her so.

And without saying anything else, we all go back to our work. No whispering. No gossip. You can almost taste the relief in the room. Something's changed. And it's definitely for the better.

"Oi, Willow," comes a voice from across the table. "You coming to sit with us or what?" It's Tay. She's smiling. And so is Nish. So I get up, pick up my page of fractions and go and sit with them.

It's as easy as that.

After

Have you ever felt like all the pieces of you are in the right place, like a Rubik's Cube when all the sides are the right colour? Have you ever felt like you know exactly what you are doing, and that what you are doing is right?

I think of Mum's images of the perfect future. Her images of me, as someone completely different, and I wonder … was that really what she wanted for me, or was it her way of trying to make everything seem like it wasn't as bad as it was?

How had we got things so wrong?

But it's never too late to make a difference. Sometimes all it takes is someone speaking up, someone doing the right thing. And that frees other people too. It turns out Marie was involved in all sorts of things. She'd been getting people to steal for her for over a year. The thing that all the kids who stole for her had in common was they were missing something. A person. A feeling. A thing. She saw people who needed help, and she used that to get them to do things they wouldn't normally do. I never knew there were people like that in the world. But I do now. I wonder how they end up like that? We haven't spoken since that evening. She's not been back to The Book Box.

Part of me can't help but wonder if she's OK. I know I'd choose to be me over Marie, any day.

Mum and I are standing beside Nanna's grave. It's the first time we've been here together since the funeral. I remember that day like it was yesterday. Mum, dressed in black, with a little veil over her face, just like in an old movie. Not saying anything. Not doing anything. Not taking my hand when I reached out to squeeze it. I think we both closed off after that.

"Hi, Nanna," I say, pulling out the flask of tea and two mugs, my Crunchie one, and one that says *Mum* on the side of it in purple letters that I bought Mum from the pound shop. And of course, Nanna's special cup and saucer from the set she and Grandad were given for their wedding day. I lay the blanket out on the grass. They've cut it and it's all neat. Mum and I sit down next to each other as I pour out the tea and Mum breaks the chocolate into pieces.

"Hi, Mum," says Mum.

The air is fresh in that way spring is. The smell of petals, and cold air laced with a bit of sun. We are both in coats, and hats. It's not warm at all really. But we pretend it is as we start to sip our tea, and watch Nanna's cup, the tea rippling slightly, as though she is breathing on it. As though she is there.

"Well, this is nice," says Mum, and smiles.

"It is," I say.

"I'm glad you convinced me to come."

I've talked to Nanna like she is still alive, and can still hear me, and like she's my best friend in the whole world, which it always felt she was, and would be. I didn't know how much I missed her. And I didn't know how much Mum acting like she didn't miss her made me feel like she was disappearing. That she was gone, even more than she really was.

Mum speaks a bit louder as though she's talking to Nanna. "I'm sorry I haven't been, Mum. I meant to come sooner. I didn't know how."

That is surprisingly honest for Mum. I'm impressed. A lot has happened since the day I did my speech at The Book Box. When Jed and Rox spoke to Mum about what had happened she was so shocked. She didn't know what to do or say. "Are you really that unhappy, darling?" she'd said, and reached out for an actual cuddle.

"I was," I said. "But I feel a bit better now."

Rich had been upset about the necklace. But we've been talking it through. He was only upset that I couldn't talk to him. As I brought the necklace back, it was only missing for a few days. But. It will take time for him to trust me again, and I'm OK with that. Some things you can't rush. I'm glad he's moving in. We're all going to look at houses next week, after the new tenants move into Nanna's.

"Nanna knows," I say.

"I know," says Mum quietly, popping a piece of chocolate into her mouth. "I'm really sorry, Willow."

"What about?"

"Pretending I was OK to everyone else. That put a lot of pressure on you."

"Ah, I didn't mind," I say. But. I suppose I did, really. "It wasn't nice, always," I add. Because I'm trying to be more honest about my feelings. It's not always easy.

"Yes, you did," says Mum. "I was so worried about losing things, I didn't notice what was right under my nose."

"Nanna loved that phrase."

"She did."

"I really miss her," I say.

"Oh, darling, so do I. Very much." And we hug again. Mum moves over on the blanket, right over, right next to me, and puts her arms around me, pulling my face to her chest and just ... squeezes. Just the right amount. I thought I wasn't someone who likes hugs. But maybe somewhere along the line, me and Mum stopped hugging because ... we didn't know how to? I'd hug her every day if it felt like this, I realise. I really would.

We are both crying now. We've not cried together since the day Mum got the phone call to say Nanna had died. It was like somebody turned off a switch to stop us feeling bad feelings. But it stopped me feeling other things too. It stopped me feeling happiness, and hope, and it stopped me feeling like myself. I not only missed Nanna. I missed Mum. And I'd missed myself.

"Right," says Mum, pulling away, her mascara in big black smudges down her cheeks that she doesn't even try to wipe away. "We'd better make sure you're not late for *High Society*."

Is it that time already? I don't want this moment to end. I want to sit with Mum, right here, like this, for always. How do we all cope with knowing nothing lasts forever? Some things should last forever. Like love. And kindness. And cuddles.

We put away the tea things. I take a final slurp of mine, and Mum pours Nanna's next to the grave, like I always do.

"I hope I've made it right, Mum," says Mum. "I know you've always been very particular about your tea." We both laugh then. It's true. Nanna only really liked tea that she made herself. But we will do our best.

We don't speak in the car, but Mum puts her hand on my knee, and I let it stay there. It feels warm. Her fingers are like words, but better. I didn't realise how important it is to have someone comfort you. To feel near to. Like cubs with their mothers, curled up, safe.

Mum drops me off at the Arts Centre and I walk in proudly, excited. I show my tickets. Two. But I'm here by myself. There's a seat for Nanna, and I buy her a programme and put it on her seat next to me. I suddenly remember the film we saw the first time she ever took me to the cinema. It was *Frozen*. I was so small, and the chair seemed to engulf me. She held my hand all the way through. And she said, "Well, look there. A good story with no romance at the centre. I like that. And I like that snowman."

I liked those things too. And the music. It felt like electricity going through me.

High Society comes up on the screen, in the loopy font they were so fond of back in those days. I feel happy. I thought I needed a friend to come to the cinema with but I didn't. I like being by myself. Old films are something I shared with Nanna and that never has to stop. She is with me whenever I watch them, or think about them, or hum along to them when I'm tidying my room, when I'm drawing in my notebook, when I'm making notes for the blog I'm going to write one day.

I don't have to do things differently. My favourite outfit *is* my grey tracksuit bottoms and the oversized green jumper with the cheeseburger wearing sunglasses on it. I like plain cheese sandwiches. I like my own company and looking up the history of cinema. I like the lake at the park, watching the ripples when it rains, lots and lots of tiny taps and swirls. I don't really *want* anything more than what I've got right now. And I like it. I don't have to change. I can do things alone, and that's OK.

I like doing things alone. Just not all the time.

The film starts. I put a toffee into my mouth. I'm meeting Tay and Nish after at the Radley for a milkshake. Then we're going roller skating. I actually think I'm ready for proper friends. And I'm ready to not be better, or be different, or be a great success, or impressive. Or anything, really. I'm just ready to just be me.

Acknowledgements

Thank you to all the people I'm lucky enough to have in my life that support my writing and were there during the writing of this book.

Thank you to Jo Unwin for being the best agent and much more than that. I feel lucky to know you. Thank you to my editor Fiona Scoble at Nosy Crow. It was a pleasure to work with you and you really did help make this book the best version of itself. Thank you!

Thank you to all the team at Nosy Crow. I love having my books published with you. Thanks to Tom Bonnick too, who believed in this book back when it was only a few paragraphs long.

Thank you to Alexandra Benedict, Alice Broadway, Owen Booth, Tim Clare, Netti Finney, Sarah Hillary, Rachael Lucas, Erin Kelly, Niki Mackay, Holly Seddon, Becca Staples, Keris Stainton, Jade Tucker, Shelley Valdivia, Wendy Vaizey, Debbie Williamson, Jade Willis-Dawson, Rebecca Winward who all, maybe knowing it and maybe not, supported me in different ways while I was writing this book.

Thank you, Cassie Crane, Em Hardy, Gareth

Hardy and Kaye Read. I appreciate you all very much.

Thanks to my sister Jodie Webster. Ah man. The first person I made up stories for and who I love and appreciate very much. To Hollie, Jake, Noah and Dexter. I consider myself a very lucky auntie.

Thank you, Nick, for the laptop I did the rewrites on and for memories going back to 1988.

Thank you to all the children and staff at Fakenham Junior School where I worked when I came up with the idea for this book. What a wonderful place to teach and be it was for me. Thank you.

Thank you to Heidi Davies and all the brilliant staff and pupils at Brimpton C of E Primary School.

Thank you Nell. I hope you know how loved you are. And that you being in the world makes it a better place. And that I have always admired your ability to be yourself. Keep that up, some people never get there. I love you very much. Equally. More. Infinity. Plus 1.

And thank you to all the readers of my books. You keep helping make my childhood dreams come true.